A Candlelight Ecstasy Classic Romance

"DO YOU KEEP YOUR BARGAINS, HUNTER?" STACY ASKED VERY QUIETLY.

"Will you really keep your claws off my brother and his wife if I marry you?"

"Yes, Stacy Rylan," he whispered. "I keep my bargains. As long as you stay married to me, your brother and his wife are safe."

"Regardless of how satisfied or unsatisfied you may be with the pact afterward? Regardless of the success of your revenge?"

"You have my word," he said with arrogance.

"Won't you give me some idea of how long you intend to waste both our lives in this stupid venture? Six months? A year? What will it take to satisfy you?"

"You want to know the limit on your prison sentence?"

"It's customary."

"What if I said I had no intention of ever dissolving the marriage?" he murmured, his eyes raking her.

CANDLELIGHT ECSTASY CLASSIC ROMANCES

MORGAN WADE'S WOMAN, *Amii Lorin*
MARRIAGE TO A STRANGER, *Dorothy Phillips*
THE SHADOWED REUNION, *Lillian Cheatham*
A WAITING GAME, *Diana Blayne*

CANDLELIGHT ECSTASY ROMANCES®

BARGAIN WITH THE DEVIL

Jayne Castle

A CANDLELIGHT ECSTASY CLASSIC ROMANCE

Published by
Dell Publishing Co., Inc.
1 Dag Hammarskjold Plaza
New York, New York 10017

Dell ® TM 681510, Dell Publishing Co., Inc.

A Candlelight Ecstasy Classic Romance

Candlelight Ecstasy Romance®, 1,203,540, is a registered
trademark of Dell Publishing Co., Inc.

ISBN: 0-440-10423-8

Printed in the United States of America

One Previous Edition

September 1987

10 9 8 7 6 5 4 3 2 1

WFH

To Our Readers:

As of September 1987, Candlelight Romances will cease publication of Candlelight Ecstasies and Supremes. The editors of Candlelight would like to thank our readers for 20 years of loyalty and support. Providing quality romances has been a wonderful experience for us and one we will cherish. Again, from everyone at Candlelight, thank you!

Sincerely,

The Editors

BARGAIN WITH THE DEVIL

CHAPTER ONE

If they had been filming a western that night in Tucson instead of throwing an elegant party, Stacy Rylan knew which role Hunter Manning would have been playing. He would have been the man wearing the black hat.

She stood perfectly still in the shadows of the patio, a half-eaten apple clutched in one hand, and watched Hunter deliberately try to seduce her sister-in-law. A very dangerous man, Stacy told herself nervously as the fingers of the hand not holding the apple curled into her palm in silent frustration. Dangerous because there was no real passion or even elemental desire in Manning's approach. Couldn't Leana see that? Everything about the man was cold and calculating. Stacy shivered involuntarily as Hunter whispered something in a low growl of a voice that caused Leana to giggle delightedly.

"I really should be getting back to our guests," Leana murmured, a trace of genuine anxiety in the soft, lovely smile she turned upward to Hunter.

"So soon?" Hunter said, sounding regretful. He stood with his back toward the watching Stacy, casually bracing his tall, lean frame against one of the posts that supported the latticework patio roof. Pale light spilled from the open doors of the house and gave the almost-black hair of his attentively bent head a dark, sinister gleam. He had apparently shed his jacket earlier, as had every other man at the party in deference to the balmy Tucson night, and the crisp whiteness of his well-tailored shirt seemed to accent the dark hardness Stacy sensed in the man. Good lord! she scolded herself ruefully. She hadn't even met Hunter Manning yet and already she was prepared to forgo that dubious pleasure. If only he would leave Leana alone!

"I'm afraid I must," Leana whispered in response to Hunter's query, tipping her beautiful blond head back to meet his eyes. Stacy could cheerfully have kicked her lovely young sister-in-law at that moment. Leana might be only twenty-three and rather spoiled, but she's a married woman who ought to know better than to allow herself to be caught up in this sort of situation.

"You'll come back to me later?" Hunter asked in a low, demanding tone that could have passed for passion but didn't to Stacy's ears.

"I'll—I'll try," Leana promised, her blue eyes flickering with the excitement of a child who has found a new toy. "Now I really must go." She made to turn away, her body slim and graceful in the expensive silk dress Stacy knew she had bought only yesterday, but Hunter put out a large hand and caught her gently by the chin.

"A little something to remember me by," he told Leana and, shifting slightly, dropped a rather casual kiss on the pretty young woman's petite nose.

Leana smiled and then turned, disappearing quickly back toward the house and her guests. Stacy grimaced, forced to admire Hunter's methods even while she deplored them. A full, passionate kiss on the lips would probably have frightened Leana, who was clearly a little nervous about the flirtation, but the light, unaggressive caress Hunter had delivered was perfectly calculated to entice without making the girl any more anxious.

12

For a moment longer Stacy stood silently watching as Hunter stared after Leana. His back was still turned toward her, and Stacy knew she could simply wait in the shadows until he chose to rejoin the other guests. He need never know his little game had a witness. That would be the safer course of action, Stacy knew instinctively. Better by far not to get involved with this man, let alone do something foolish like confronting him. But something had to be done, and she was very much afraid that telling her brother what was going on would accomplish little. Eric was hopelessly in love with his spoiled, lovely wife, and he was hopelessly inundated with the task of learning what it meant to be president of Rylan Enterprises. He would choose to believe Leana was merely being friendly to a business associate, and he would most certainly be annoyed at Stacy for implying his wife was heading for trouble. Stacy deliberated the situation a second longer and then she made up her mind.

The first thing she did was to take a large, crunching bite out of the apple she held.

While it could not be said that Hunter appeared terribly startled by the sound, Stacy knew she had his complete and very alert attention. He didn't move away from his negligent stance against the post, and his arms remained folded against the expanse of his chest, but the dark head turned so that the strong chin was aligned with his shoulder, and he waited with an easy patience for whoever was behind him to announce his or her presence. The strange streak of silver in his hair was suddenly visible.

It was the first time Stacy had been given a clear glimpse of his profile, and what she saw confirmed her earlier impression that Hunter Manning could have played the role of outlaw with little or no theatrical assistance. Every line in his face, from the deep-set eyes, the arrogant blade

13

of a nose, and the harshly carved cheekbones declared to the world that this was a man who lived by his own rules. A man who, if he had lived in the Tucson of a hundred years earlier, would have worn a gun slung low on his narrow hip and strapped professionally to his thigh. There was a grim, no-nonsense line to his mouth, which made one instinctively wary, Stacy decided, chewing absently on the bite of apple. The overall effect of Hunter Manning's strong, uncompromising features seemed curiously accented by the silvery streak in the near-blackness of his hair. It began at the low side part and swept across, a section of a lock that would fall forward over his brow if his hair were to become tousled. Stacy sighed inwardly, acknowledging that she'd probably made a serious mistake and telling herself bracingly that she was committed now.

"She's married," Stacy announced baldly, unable to think of any other way to begin the confrontation.

"I'm aware of that." Hunter's hard mouth quirked upward in a chilling, challenging way, and he slowly swiveled to face his accuser. "The fact, however, is a matter that concerns only myself and the lady involved." The cool edge on his words would have effectively deterred Stacy under other conditions.

"Her husband," she stated clearly, grateful for the poor protection of the shadows, "is my brother."

One heavy black brow lifted with a surprising degree of interest. "You're a Rylan?" Hunter asked, dropping his hands to his side and taking a couple of deceptively casual steps toward the spot where Stacy stood beneath the shelter of a shade tree.

Stacy frowned, aware of the sardonic gray gaze that was sweeping her from head to foot. Suddenly the shadows were providing very little protection. A fine time to

14

become style conscious, she told herself with grim humor, aware of the rather untidy and overly casual sight she presented. "I'm Stacy Rylan," she announced proudly, lifting her chin.

"Interesting," Hunter drawled, his gaze focusing first on the precariously perched knot of heavy dark brown hair with its almost buried red hints. Several strands of the stuff were straggling free of confinement. "I didn't know there was a sister."

Stacy's frown deepened as the fog-colored eyes took in her jeans and bright flower-patterned cotton shirt. She was wearing leather sandals, and not one piece of jewelry to soften the overall effect. Well, she wasn't at this party to socialize, she reminded herself, and it didn't matter in the least what Hunter Manning thought of her appearance! Besides, if he preferred his women petite and soft and lovely, nothing Stacy could have worn would have sufficiently changed her enough to meet with Manning's approval. She was definitely not another Leana! A straightforward, rather than flirtatious, expression was mirrored in wide green eyes, which watched the world with humor and intelligence. Stacy knew her features were not unattractive, but there was a certain basic, healthy wholesomeness about them that kept the straight little nose, firm jawline, and pleasantly curved lips from being seductive or coy. Leana was always telling her she ought to wear more makeup, but at twenty-seven, Stacy, who had never gotten into the habit, decided it was too late to start. Her figure was slim and firm, but the small, high breasts and narrow waist lacked anything resembling voluptuousness. Instead there was a sense of inner energy about her body and a supple strength, which came from the outdoor work she did.

"Now that you know there is a sister," Stacy began

15

pointedly, deliberately trying to bring his attention back from his critical perusal of her person, "you'll understand my interest in the fact that you're flirting with Leana."

Hunter met her severe glance, and the curious quirk of his mouth lifted higher as if he found her amusing. "Leana appears to be quite adult. Old enough to make her own decisions, I'd say," he drawled.

Stacy took another bite out of her apple, crunching thoughtfully as she considered how best to handle this man. "I'm afraid that's the problem," she said finally. "Leana really isn't all that grown-up. Not yet. She's a bit spoiled, you see, and she's quite young in many ways." The first pitch, Stacy decided carefully, would be to Hunter's better instincts. If he had any.

"You mean she's a little flirt," Hunter said, nodding agreeably.

"I didn't say that!" Stacy snapped around the mouthful of apple. The fruit was beginning to play the same role as a cigarette might have played in the hands of a smoker. It gave her something to do and thus helped hide her growing nervousness. "It's just that my brother has been terribly busy lately and Leana—"

"Leana is starting to look elsewhere for her entertainment," Hunter concluded bluntly.

"With a little help from you, apparently!"

"I'm always happy to oblige a beautiful woman," Hunter retorted silkily.

"There are a number of them here tonight," Stacy shot back meaningfully. "Why don't you go back inside and have a look around?"

"Sorry, but Leana is the one who offers me what I'm looking for at the moment," he said smoothly. "She's one of you."

"One of us?" Stacy gasped, uncomprehending. "What in the world are you talking about?"

"She's a Rylan," Hunter informed her in a simple, deadly tone.

Stacy chilled, appalled by the coldness of his narrowed, fog-colored eyes. "What's that got to do with anything?" she whispered.

"Do you know who I am?" he asked almost pleasantly.

"You're Hunter Manning," Stacy managed, the apple forgotten for the moment. "Leana told me you'd be here tonight. She . . . she described you quite accurately."

"That was the first you'd heard of me?" he persisted coolly.

"I'm sorry if you feel I should know you by reputation," Stacy retorted with a hint of impatience. "But I don't normally attend my brother's parties. I'm only here tonight because I helped Leana with the flower arrangements earlier and accidentally left something behind. I was just going to slip in the back entrance and get it when I saw you here on the patio with Leana."

"Tell me something, Stacy Rylan," Hunter bit out quietly. "How old are you?"

"What the hell does that have to do with anything?" she challenged, abruptly flustered. Nothing about this little scene was making any sense!

"Twenty-six? Twenty-seven?" he hazarded calmly, studying her features with dispassionate interest.

"I'm twenty-seven, although I don't see why it should matter to you!" she snapped angrily.

"So you would have been about thirteen at the time." He nodded to himself. "Too young and much too sheltered to take an interest in your father's business activities!"

"Mr. Manning," Stacy began feelingly, "will you kindly

explain your point? I'm afraid I've lost the thread of the conversation!"

"With pleasure, Miss Rylan." He smiled very dangerously. "Soon all the Rylans will be aware of me. There's no reason you shouldn't be the first. I'm not here tonight for business or social reasons, although your brother thinks I am."

"You're here to seduce my sister-in-law?" Stacy breathed tightly, her mind floundering for some rational explanation of this man's behavior.

"It seemed an appropriate place to start," he agreed with a mocking tilt of his head.

"To start what?" Stacy demanded in a curious mixture of anger and fear.

"My revenge, of course," he answered as calmly as if remarking on the weather.

"Your revenge!" Stacy stared unbelievingly up at the tall, remote-faced stranger, her shock clearly reflected in the wide green eyes and slightly parted lips. "For what? I don't understand. Leana says you only moved to Tucson a couple of months ago. What could my family possibly have done to you in that time?"

"What your family did to me occurred fourteen years ago," Hunter told her grimly. "I was twenty at the time, and I made a promise to myself that one day I would return. It took quite awhile, Stacy Rylan, but I'm here and I'm going to finish what I set out to do. Fourteen years it's taken to put together a company successful enough to allow me to return to Arizona and meet Paul J. Rylan on an equal level. But two months ago I finally moved into the house I'd had built for me last winter in the foothills, and I'm here to stay until I've satisfied myself!"

Stacy flinched from the harsh determination in his words. She didn't doubt him for one single moment. This man was bent on revenge, and she didn't think there was much that could stop him!

"What—what was it my family did to you?" she whispered, her mouth dry with dread.

"Your father ruined mine. Very simply and very efficiently." Hunter grated starkly.

Stacy licked her lips unconsciously. "How?" she whispered helplessly.

"The mechanics of it were rather involved." Hunter shrugged. "But it amounted to a takeover. A takeover in which even the courtesy of retaining the former management was ignored! My father spent his life building the electronics firm that is now part of Rylan Enterprises. Losing it was like losing his whole reason for living. He died a year after the takeover." There was a strangely unemotional bitterness in the words as Hunter faced Stacy and told her the tale.

"That—that sounds a little oversimplified," Stacy began bravely, sensing some need to defend her father. "I'm sure there was a great deal more to it than that. Business can be very complex. . . ."

"Oh, there was a great deal more to it," he agreed at once. "There was, for example, the day I came to your father's house and pleaded with him not to go through with the deal. You and your brother weren't there at the time, but your mother was. I remember the way she looked at me as if pitying me, but she made no effort to change your father's mind!"

"What did my father say?" Stacy demanded softly.

"Business, he said, was business," Hunter quoted casually.

Stacy took a deep breath. She could almost hear her father saying just those words. Paul Rylan was a businessman down to his fingertips. "Your quarrel, if you really

19

think you have one, would seem to be with my father, Mr. Manning," she stated, wondering at the depths of a revenge that could ride a man for fourteen years. A part of her wanted to reach out and tell him she understood, but the lines were clearly drawn in this engagement. As a Rylan, there was no question about which side she represented. Hunter Manning would not welcome her sympathy, and he certainly wouldn't allow it to deflect him from his path. The only thing Stacy could hope to do was mediate to some slight degree. "If you're determined to take up this matter again after all this time, then it should be with Dad. And for that you'll have to wait," she continued hopefully. "My parents are on an extended cruise. They won't return for a month!"

"I know where your parents are." Hunter half-smiled. "I made it my business to find out as soon as I moved to Tucson. It makes no difference. I intend to repay him in the same way he treated my father. Paul Rylan is going to watch helplessly as something and someone he cares about is ruined."

"You're going to try and buy out Rylan Enterprises?" Stacy asked, startled at the audacity of the move.

"No, I have no wish to acquire possession of your father's business," Hunter drawled. "I have other plans."

"Just where does Leana fit into your 'plans'?" Stacy demanded.

"Your brother, as you mentioned, is very much in love with his new wife," Hunter commented. "It's no great secret."

"Yes." Stacy waited fearfully for the next statement.

"Seducing her will serve quite well to take his mind off the business of running Rylan Enterprises, don't you think?" Hunter went on thoughtfully.

Stacy blanched. "He's just taken on the job," she whis-

20

pered. "My father turned the position over to him only a few months ago!"

"After grooming him quite carefully for years. Quite an investment in time and effort your father has made. The same sort of investment my father made."

"My brother had nothing to do with what happened fourteen years ago," Stacy hissed. "You have no right to take out your revenge on him."

"Business is business."

"Oh, shut up! You can't just casually set about seducing Leana merely to hurt my brother and weaken him so that he'll fail in running the company. It wouldn't work anyway! I'm going to tell him exactly what's going on!"

"He won't believe you until it's too late. Leana certainly isn't going to confirm your tale. In fact, if you take that approach, I'll simply arrange for sweet little Leana to feel that I'm the persecuted one in the story. Before she knows what's happened, she'll find herself on my side. Your brother, fool that he is, will try to placate her rather than make a scene. He'll be too afraid of driving her away. But he'll start worrying about Leana's 'friendship' with me. By the time he has the guts to do anything about it, it will be too late." There was a menacing satisfaction in Hunter's smile now. "The whole Rylan family will be humiliated. Your brother will be crushed, and your father will be furious. Paul Rylan will also be quite helpless. It will be amusing to see if he comes to plead with me to leave Leana alone!"

"No!" Stacy exclaimed, totally outraged now. "You can't do this!"

"Who's going to stop me?" he inquired mildly.

"Is it money you're after? Do you want my father to buy you off?"

"Money," Hunter Manning declared calmly, "is no

21

longer a problem in my life. I have all I need and the means to make more if I wish. I may not be precisely able to buy and sell Rylan Enterprises, but Manning Development Corporation can certainly hold its own when it comes to assets! The day your father comes to my home and offers to buy me off will be a fascinating one indeed. It will give me great pleasure to tell him to go to hell."

"You just want to hurt," Stacy murmured. "The way you were hurt."

"The way my father was hurt," he corrected immediately, frowning.

"Did he put this notion of revenge in your head?" Stacy asked deliberately, eyeing the set features above her.

"I told you, my father lost everything after he lost the business," Hunter growled. "He didn't even have the will to seek revenge."

"So you've appointed yourself the one to do it for him. But he's gone now, so who will appreciate your efforts?" Stacy pressed carefully.

He chuckled unexpectedly. "Don't think you're going to talk me out of this with a bit of patio psychology," he mocked. "Although you're welcome to try. After all, part of the revenge will be watching the various members of the Rylan clan grow increasingly upset and finally desperate. There are all sorts of possibilities, you know. One is that your father will fear for the health of the company and will attempt to resume control. Your brother will resent that, naturally, and they'll quarrel." Hunter lifted a hand as if handing the conclusion to Stacy on a platter. "Another wedge, this time between father and son. Your father won't like that one bit. Not after raising your brother as the heir apparent!"

Stacy thought of the proud manner in which Paul Rylan had turned the responsibility for the day-to-day running

22

of Rylan Enterprises over to her thirty-year-old brother, and then taken off on a lengthy cruise to demonstrate his complete confidence in the young man. Then she reflected on the humiliation her brother, Eric, would experience if he had to face his father with the news that the son of an old business rival had run off with his beautiful young wife, of whom Paul and Miriam Rylan had so wholeheartedly approved! If there were problems with the business on top of that . . . !

"Your whole plan hinges on Leana going along with your seduction routine," Stacy snapped. "She's not a vicious person. I think she really does care for my brother. I'll explain what you're up to, and she won't have anything further to do with you!"

"You think not? As long as your brother is too tied up with business or too doting on his little flirt of a wife to take her in hand, I'll be able to control Leana!"

Stacy was very much afraid he was right. The pressures of business at the moment were such that Eric simply didn't have time to do all the amusing and entertaining things with his wife that Leana expected as her due. Furthermore, he tended to give his charming new bride everything she wished, including her way in a great many things. Hunter probably didn't know it, but there had already been quarrels between the recently married pair. Even Stacy wasn't certain how deep or how brutal the arguments had been. She perceived only a hint of them from the few things Leana had casually mentioned. Hunter's efforts might find particularly wide opportunity if he really set out to break up Eric and Leana's marriage. Stacy glanced down at the partially eaten apple in her hand, trying to think of some way to talk Hunter Manning out of his plans. Slowly she lifted her head, meeting the hard gray gaze with an honest, pleading expression in her own green eyes.

"Mr. Manning," she began clearly, deliberately. "I understand that you were very affected by what happened fourteen years ago, but revenge is a dangerous emotion if you let it dominate your life. What happiness will it bring you to destroy my brother's marriage?"

"I'm not looking for happiness, Miss Rylan," Hunter returned mockingly. "Merely satisfaction."

"And what will you do when you have that? Do you suppose it will last very long?"

"Longer than what most people call happiness, I believe," he told her arrogantly.

"You can't have known much happiness, I think," Stacy mused gently.

"Thank you for your concern, Miss Rylan. I assure you it's entirely unnecessary!"

"I agree! I expect you're the last person in the world over whom I should worry! I only mentioned it because I thought you might want to consider the relative merits of happiness and the satisfaction of revenge. I think if you gain one, it will be at the expense of the other, and you ought to consider the long-range consequences!" Stacy retorted spiritedly.

"I'm fully capable of doing my own long-range planning, thank you. I have, after all, just spent fourteen years getting myself to the precise point where I am today."

Stacy sighed, shaking her head in a small, negative gesture that loosened a few more tendrils of the topknot. "There's nothing I can say that will make you change your mind?"

"Nothing," he assured her with a certain relish. "But I'm enjoying hearing you try!"

"I'll bet you are," she breathed tightly.

"A form of happiness, Miss Rylan," he persisted coolly. "You should be glad you're its source!"

She flushed. "What a nasty man you are. Nasty and arrogant and ruthless! If your father was anything like you, I can't say I feel any sympathy for—" She broke off, startled as Hunter moved with the lightning swiftness of a large, sleekly muscled cat, catching her wrist and causing her to drop the apple she'd been holding. She glared at him, unprepared for the small act of violence and annoyed with herself for not having kept more distance between them.

"Don't say it, Stacy Rylan," he ordered in a rasping tone that was sharp enough to cut glass and certainly sharp enough to make Stacy regret her impulsive words. "You can attack me all you like, but don't you dare say anything about my father. You know nothing of the situation or the kind of man he was!" The hard fingers wrapped around her wrist tightened threateningly until Stacy, guided by feminine instinct, nodded her head in submission, saying nothing. He held her for a second longer, and she stood very still, tensely waiting for him to release his hold on her. Then he let go of her as swiftly and unexpectedly as he had grabbed her.

"That's better," he approved, watching with a total lack of repentance as she rubbed her reddened wrist automatically. "It may take some time, but one by one I shall make certain all the Rylans have cause to remember me!"

"My father and brother will find a way to deal with you," Stacy vowed through gritted teeth.

"I doubt it, and even if, in the end, they manage to get rid of me, I'll have had my revenge."

Desperately Stacy sought for another approach. "If you're so bent on revenge against the Rylans, it's hardly fair to use Leana! She's only a very recently married and very vulnerable young woman. Surely you can find a way to get what you want without using her!"

"She's a Rylan now," he tossed back uncaringly. "I see nothing wrong in using her—"

"Nothing wrong!" Stacy yelped, incensed. "What's the matter with you? Are you totally without any morality? Leana has only been married to my brother for a few short months! You can't possibly justify using her and then discarding her like an old doll!" She'd struck some sort of nerve with that last statement, Stacy was sure of it. The only evidence was the slight narrowing of the gray gaze, and the tightened mouth, but she sensed a weakening in his resolve. All she had to do was find a way to capitalize on that small weakening.

"There's no point in trying to make me change my mind. It's been made up for a long time!" Hunter told her roughly.

"I'm only trying to make you see that you shouldn't involve my sister-in-law," Stacy said quickly. "You could ruin her life. Think of some other way to attack the Rylans! An honorable way!"

"Honorable! What does a Rylan know about honor?" he scoffed in a low fury. "Business is the only thing that ever counted with your father, and I have no doubt but that the credo runs in the family. Don't lecture me about honor, Miss Rylan!"

"But that's just exactly what I'm doing," she slung back immediately. "I've told you before, your quarrel is with my father, and you have no right to be attacking my brother and his wife!"

"If the only way I can get at your father is through his son, that's what I'm going to do." There was a rawness in Hunter's words that told its own story. He was an angry man who had come too far to turn away from his goal, even if he realized he was in the wrong. There was only one way out of all this, Stacy realized suddenly. One way out for her brother and for this man driven by revenge. She must offer him another target.

"For a man who has spent fourteen years building a business empire the size of Manning Development Corporation, you're rather blind to your options," she taunted quite bravely, her head held high.

"Is that right?" he retorted smoothly, clearly regaining control of his emotions. Stacy wondered at the speed with which he managed the feat. The rawness and anger had vanished almost instantly from his deep voice. "First I get lectures on honor, and now I'm to be favored with one on business options. By all means continue, Miss Rylan. I'm fascinated!"

Stacy felt her own anger welling up inside and deliberately quelled the sensation. She must remain quite cool about this or it wouldn't stand a chance of working. Surely she'd long since mastered her fiery temperament!

"It's very simple, really. You said yourself that one effective way of attacking my father is through his children. But Eric isn't his only child, Mr. Manning!"

There was an unbelievably tense moment of silence as Hunter stared at her with a hooded gaze. Stacy would have given a fortune to know exactly what was going through his mind in that moment. Instead she was forced to wait with an appearance of outward calm for his response. It seemed a very long time before he slowly inclined his head in a mocking acknowledgment of her rash statement.

"You're suggesting I use Paul Rylan's daughter. You." Hunter said the words with a peculiar flatness that Stacy couldn't begin to understand.

"Why not?" she managed politely, although the question took all her courage. "As the only daughter in the family, I surely represent a vulnerable point to my parents." She was skating on terribly thin ice. Her only hope lay in the fact that until tonight Hunter hadn't even known of her existence. He couldn't possibly know about her relationship with her parents!

There was another painfully tense silence while Hunter seemed to consider her words. "What exactly are you suggesting, Miss Rylan?" he finally asked evenly, almost brutally.

Stacy swallowed, aware of a faint trembling in her limbs. She must not betray her anxiety. "I would have thought that a man who was capable of dreaming up that sordid little plot with Leana would be able to concoct something suitable involving me!" She would be as cool as he was!

"Something suitably sordid you mean?" he asked dangerously. The near-black hair gleamed once again in the dim light as he put out a hand and ran thumb and forefinger along the line of her jaw to her throat.

Without a word Stacy held her ground, refusing to flinch as his fingers came to a halt on the pulse. She knew he could sense its rapid movement.

"Nervous?" he chided softly. "Afraid that I'll take you up on your so generous offer? It's not a bad idea, I think. There are a number of interesting possibilities. But I want to hear your idea in its entirety first! Tell me what you're proposing, Stacy Rylan. Tell me exactly what you're offering."

It occurred to Stacy that his demand was, in itself, a part of a new form of revenge. He was going to try and humiliate her by making her spell out precisely what she was willing to do to keep him from attacking her brother's marriage. Well, if he thought she wouldn't have the fortitude to go through with it, he was wrong, she told herself fiercely. She had spent the better part of her life insisting on making her own decisions and abiding by them. She was prepared to abide by this one, too!

"Isn't it obvious?" she asked in a soft, biting voice. "I'm offering you the chance to pretend you're having an affair with Paul Rylan's daughter! What better revenge could you have? Don't you imagine my father would be furious if he thought you were using me just to get even with him? You could make it quite clear to him that that was your only interest in me!"

"An affair with Rylan's daughter," Hunter murmured thoughtfully, his fingers at her throat curving slightly to encircle the smooth column of skin. The gray eyes poured over her taut features in a wave of fog that left Stacy feeling marooned on a chartless sea. "Yes," he nodded finally, "that probably would infuriate Paul Rylan. But it would only work if the daughter cooperated! I wonder. Would you cooperate, Stacy Rylan?" Very deliberately Hunter trailed the tips of his fingers down to the small bones at the hollows of her shoulders. When she didn't move, he went further, as if testing her will. His large hand began moving down the small slope of one breast.

It was too much. With a small gasp of outrage Stacy stepped backward, only to be brought up short by the trunk of the tree under which she had been sheltering. "I said you could 'pretend' to have an affair with me," she reminded him furiously as his hand dropped back to his side. "And, yes, I'll go along with the pretense. But that's all!"

"What would I want with something as unsatisfying as a phony love affair?" Hunter inquired coolly, closing the small distance between them with one step.

"You couldn't possibly have any interest in a—a genu-

29

ine relationship," Stacy whispered desperately. "I'm not your sort at all!"

"Perhaps a man in pursuit of revenge would be able to overlook small details like that!" He half-smiled in a challenging fashion that made Stacy more nervous than ever. "How far will you go to protect your brother and your father, Stacy Rylan?"

CHAPTER TWO

"You can't be serious!" Stacy finally breathed, feeling horribly trapped between the solid tree trunk and the equally solid length of Hunter Manning's lean, dynamic frame. He was waiting for her answer, she knew. Waiting to see how far she would sink her pride to protect her family.

"I can tell you right now that your offer of a fake affair doesn't particularly interest me," he said coldly, not touching her again but standing far too close for any degree of comfort. "You'll have to do better than that, I'm afraid. Try something else, my little bargainer."

"I don't believe you truly want an affair with me," Stacy declared staunchly, her fingers instinctively going to the open collar of her shirt in a small gesture of anxiety. "You've said revenge against my father is your goal. My offer would allow you that revenge. You have no right to ask for anything more!"

"You're not going to reopen that subject again, are you?" he asked with a dry chuckle. "I'll exercise whatever rights I please in this matter. I've waited far too long for my revenge to let myself be swayed by moral arguments. Can't you get that through your head, lady?"

"What do you want me to say?" Stacy hissed. "That I'll agree to sleep with you if you'll leave Leana and Eric alone?"

"Yes. I want to hear you say that," he growled in sudden harshness, leaning forward and putting a hand on the tree trunk beside her head. His rugged, intense face was so close to hers, it must have looked from a distance as if he were about to kiss her, Stacy thought wildly.

"All right," she heard herself say on such a thin thread of sound, she wondered if she'd spoken aloud. What was she doing? This couldn't be her making such a rash statement! "I'll agree to what you ask. But you must give me your word you won't attempt to use Eric and Leana in your revenge. Only me!" Later, she promised herself passionately, later she would figure a way out of this bizarre situation. There had to be a way out! It was vital to focus this man's attention strictly on herself and her father. Between the two of them they could deal with Hunter Manning. For now it was imperative to protect the most vulnerable members of the family. The green eyes flared with her inner resolve as she faced her tormentor.

"Ah!" Hunter snarled very gently, making no secret of his intent study of her drawn face. "Things are going along very nicely, indeed, aren't they? I have barely begun my campaign and already I have the daughter of the house offering herself to me." Abruptly he straightened and turned away from her. He didn't move far, but his back was once again to her and Stacy began to breath more normally. Now what? she wondered in the agonizing silence. What would happen next? The sense of danger around her seemed almost palpable as she waited for Hunter's acceptance or rejection of her plan. Stacy could not have said for certain which way she wanted him to go just then. Motionless, she awaited his verdict.

"I find your offer insufficient," he finally stated, still not looking at her. His attention seemed focused on the cacti collection across the patio.

Stacy took a breath and sagged against the tree in curious relief. It wasn't over, she reminded herself bitterly. In fact, she was back where she had started. Why this sense of having had one hell of a narrow escape? Desperately she tried to marshal her thoughts to present another coherent argument to dissuade him from his path, but it was difficult to think properly amidst the overwhelming relief she was experiencing. And then his next words wiped out that temporary sensation completely.

"But you have given me an idea," Hunter said quietly. "There is something else you can offer me. Something that will upset Rylan far more than thinking you're having an affair with me!"

"What . . . what are you talking about?" Stacy demanded in a hushed tone.

"I'm talking about marriage."

"You're crazy!" Stacy yelped unthinkingly. "If you're not even interested in an affair with me, how could you possibly be interested in marriage?"

Hunter swung around and retraced his steps until he once again stood over her in the darkness, his face an unreadable mask. "Because marriage to me will deprive Paul Rylan of his daughter far more effectively than an affair," he blazed. "If you're married to me, you'll be committed to me. Your loyalty will belong to *me;* to the Manning family, or what there is left of it! Not the Rylans!"

"You're out of your mind!" Stacy flashed, appalled. "I'm not about to marry you!"

"You'd rather I continue with my seduction of Leana?" he countered coldly. "I'm quite capable of accomplishing it, you know. Your brother obviously has no notion of how to protect her. He's foolishly willing to let her go her own way until she meets with disaster. And said disaster will be waiting for her, I promise!"

Stacy reacted to his threat instinctively. Without pausing to reflect on the wisdom of her actions, she swung her hand in a short, forceful arc. The slap connected with his deeply tanned cheek in a stinging blow that jolted her. "Damn you!" she grated furiously. "Stop threatening my family!"

Immediately Hunter moved, catching hold of her shoulders with hard, heavy hands that could leave bruises, Stacy knew. "Then marry me," he ripped out, giving her a fierce little shake that totally destroyed what was left of her knot of hair. The rich brown mass tumbled down around her shoulders in a confusion of curls. Fully displayed in the dim lighting of the patio, it reflected the almost hidden touches of red, which were more apparent in open sunlight.

"Marry me," Hunter persisted, his fingers digging into the skin beneath her shirt, "and I'll stop making threats!" The gray eyes glared down at her, willing her to submit. Stacy could almost feel the chains of that willpower as if they circled and coiled around her.

"But you can't want to marry me!" she wailed. "You can't! You don't even like me. . . ."

He laughed at that. A short, mocking sound that sent chills down her spine. "Hardly an important consideration. What I want from you has nothing to do with 'liking' you! But if you go along with my plans, I'll give you my word that I'll leave Leana and Eric alone. Isn't that what you're trying to accomplish? All you have to do is take the vows that bind you to me instead of the Rylans. Become my wife, Stacy, and I'll leave your brother out of this."

"And my father?" Stacy hazarded bitterly, the line of her normally smiling mouth drawn tight.

"Your father will be told who I am. It's up to him whether or not he chooses to burden the rest of the family with the knowledge," Hunter told her arrogantly.

"My—my mother will know who you are," Stacy reminded him in a husky voice, trying without much success to think her way out of the dilemma. But it was proving impossible to concentrate with the full force of Hunter Manning bearing down on her like this!

"I doubt if she even remembers me." Hunter shrugged unconcernedly. "My guess is, your father will keep the real reason for the marriage to himself and try to pretend everything is fine on the surface. Only you and he need know how thorough the revenge really will be!"

"That will satisfy you?" Stacy asked in a hard little voice. "The knowledge that my father thinks you've deliberately 'stolen' me away from the family will be sufficient to fulfill your desire for revenge?" She faced him with a clear-eyed, straightforward look that he responded to in kind.

"Yes," he whispered in a new, low voice. "That will satisfy me."

"Very well," Stacy said, drawing a deep, steadying breath and refusing to lower her eyes. "I'll marry you." Later, she promised herself again, she would search for a way out of this incredible mess. Right now she must establish her priorities and stick by them, and the first issue at hand was to keep Hunter Manning away from Eric and Leana. She would worry about her own fortunes when the time came.

Hunter continued to gaze down at her assessingly, and then he gave a short, authoritative nod. "It's settled. We'll be married as soon as I can arrange it. We'll tell your

35

brother and Leana tonight before leaving the party. I wonder if you know what you're getting into, Stacy Rylan," he added broodingly, not yet releasing her shoulders.

"Nothing very good, I'm sure," she couldn't resist spitting back.

He almost smiled at that. She could see the near-honest humor that tugged at his mouth before it twisted in a wry expression. "You may be right. I only hope you'll keep in mind that you agreed to this marriage of your own free will . . . !"

"Hardly! I'm marrying you under duress, and we both know it. Don't pretend otherwise!" she retorted through gritted teeth.

"I'm not going to accept that as an excuse if you dare step one inch out of line," he growled warningly. "You're going to be my wife, Stacy, and that means you'll be walking a very narrow ledge. I'm not the foolish, love-blinded man your brother is at the moment. My wife will know the limits and stay within them. She will never put herself in a position such that she can be used against me as Leana seems so willing to do. As my wife, your loyalty lies completely with me. Do you understand?"

"What about you?" she taunted. "Will you be loyal to me?"

"That's in your hands, isn't it?" he mocked. "The only promise I'm making to you is to leave Leana and Eric alone."

"How long do you expect such a one-sided arrangement to last?" Stacy breathed, her head high so as not to betray the despair she was beginning to feel curling in her stomach.

"Until I'm satisfied with my revenge, of course," he drawled.

"How long will that take?" she pushed angrily.

"I don't know," he muttered frankly, applying unexpected pressure on her shoulders; pressure that brought her up against the hardness of his body with a startling impact. "Perhaps until I've taught one Stacy Rylan that she shouldn't go around slapping her future husband!"

Before Stacy could react, Hunter bent his head and took her lips in a strangely fierce possession. Stunned at the action, she found herself standing perfectly still as his mouth moved on hers, conveying his intent to claim her as surely as if he had written the words in stone and forced her to read them aloud. For a mindless instant in time she endured the bold, marauding exploration, and then the realization of what was happening flooded in and she began to struggle.

"Let go of me!" she ordered, twisting her head to one side and attempting with all her strength to free herself from his hold. She knew herself to be a strong woman, yet Hunter mastered her struggles as easily as if she were a small, defenseless thing like Leana.

"Be still!" he commanded, his voice a soft warning in her ear. She felt his powerful hands twisting themselves into her hair in a grip that threatened pain if she continued to resist. "You're going to be my wife," he reminded her grimly. "You might as well get used to acting the part! Or are you going to renege on our arrangement already? You can if you wish, Miss Rylan! It's not too late, you see. It won't take much effort at all to renew my association with Leana . . . ! Are you Rylans all alike? Only willing to make deals as long as they're in your favor?"

"Stop it!" she pleaded tightly, eyes squeezed shut against the reality of what he was saying. "I'm not backing out of this."

"Fine," he said triumphantly, his lips seeking the tip of

her ear. "Then show me what I'm going to be getting out of this!"

"The only thing I'm promising you is your revenge," Stacy whispered hoarsely. "The act of marrying me will provide you with that. You have no right to demand anything else of me!"

"Are we back to discussing rights again? Be careful, Stacy dear, or I shall grow tired of your conversation."

"Perhaps that will persuade you to end the marriage quickly!" she rallied, cruelly aware of his mouth hovering in the vicinity of her vulnerable ear.

"The only thing it will persuade me to do is make certain we have a real marriage, so that I will have something else to amuse me in the event your conversation continues to bore me."

"Hunter, please . . ."

"Stop fighting me, Stacy," he advised softly. "You've made your deal, so quit trying to modify it. Show me that you're willing to go through with it. I want to see a bit of the new Manning family loyalty, which is going to replace the old Rylan loyalty. Kiss me, Stacy. Who knows? Perhaps after you get used to it, you'll find being my wife isn't so bad. Hell, you might even learn to like it!" With that, Hunter took her lips again, his hands still holding her in place for his kiss.

There was nothing gentle or inviting about the caress, but this time, partly because of his words and partly because of his threateningly painful grasp on her hair, Stacy chose to endure it rather than continue struggling. It was better not to further antagonize him at this point, she consoled herself as she felt her lips forced apart and the soft warmth of her mouth opened for his possession. Later. . . .

"I would not have suspected a Rylan of having any

softness in her," Hunter grated hoarsely, withdrawing slightly from the captured province of her mouth. Stacy opened her eyes to find the cold gray fog of his gaze reflecting a new and perhaps more dangerous element. A very male hunger stirred there, and she was horrified to discover something very female in her was both repelled and attracted by that look.

"What's the matter, Stacy Rylan? Are you finally lost for words? Are you reaching the conclusion that you may have undertaken more than you could handle when you set out to protect the other members of the family?"

"Hunter, I—" Stacy couldn't finish the sentence. Wordlessly she stared up at him. She must not let him have full control of the situation, she realized dimly. She must maintain her dignity, at least!

With a strange little twist of his lips, a twist that meant victory, Stacy was certain, Hunter released his grip on her hair, his hands circling her wrists and lifting her arms to go around his neck.

"My little Rylan wife," he murmured, stroking the length of her slender back with a motion that pressed her tightly against him. "I'm going to make a Manning out of you," he vowed. "With every fiber of your being, you will behave first as a Manning. When there are any choices to be made, you will make them with the good of the Manning family in mind. And above all you will be loyal to your Manning husband." The dark head nodded in satisfaction. "Paul Rylan will know he has lost you to me, and he will understand that there is at long last a penalty to be paid for what he did fourteen years ago!"

With a coolly possessive air that defied her to protest, Hunter let his hands settle at Stacy's small waist and then slide upward until they came to rest just under the weight of her breasts. She sucked in her breath, not daring to move and refusing to give him the satisfaction of closing her eyes against the goading expression in his face.

"Kiss me, Stacy," he invited deliberately. "And find out what it's going to be like being a Manning woman. My woman."

For an instant longer Stacy hesitated, knowing that in the end there wasn't going to be any choice but fighting the knowledge regardless. Better to give him his kiss rather than have him force it from her, she told herself bleakly, finally standing on tiptoe to brush his hard mouth with her own soft one. As she did so, she felt his hands just under her breasts shift to cup the gently rounded globes completely. The probing, circling motion of his thumbs on the tips sent shock waves through her. The thin material of her flowered shirt and the lacy bra she wore offered little protection.

At once she sought to back away, but his fingers splayed tightly against her rib cage and held her still.

"No," he told her, resuming control of the kiss she had started, "you're committed now. There's no turning back." This time his mouth lazed over hers as if testing the waters before diving into the depths, and under the compulsion of his will, his hands, and his searching mouth, Stacy stood quiescently and wondered at the turn of fate. Sensing the fight had gone out of her for the present, Hunter at last lifted his head once more and watched her with a shuttered look.

"I think," he stated finally, "it's time we told your brother of our sudden, irresistible attraction, don't you?"

"If that's what you want," Stacy heard herself say evenly, wondering what would happen when he eventually realized that the revenge he sought was going to be vastly less painful for her father now that Eric and Leana were no longer the instruments of that revenge. Would she be able to keep him from discovering how drastically she had muted his actions? Stacy asked herself. Would Hunter question the stoic, perhaps total lack of concern with which Paul Rylan was sure to greet the news of his daughter's wedding? Or would he simply assume her father was hiding his feelings, confident in the knowledge that his reasoning was correct and that Paul would be infuriated by the announcement? Since until tonight Hunter hadn't even been aware of her existence, there was no way he could know that Paul Rylan had given up on his stubborn, willful, independent daughter long ago: that both father and mother had focused the majority of their affection and approval on the son who was to inherit the family business —the son who had made the proper social marriage and who had striven hard to be worthy of his parents' respect. Stacy was certain that Leana had become the close, confiding daughter Miriam Rylan wanted. The daughter who excelled at all the social niceties and who made such an attractive member of the family. If Hunter ever realized how little real revenge he was exacting . . . ! Stacy shivered.

"Yes," Hunter said, half to himself. "It's what I want. Come along, Stacy Rylan, and let's announce the news of our unexpected engagement!" He flung an arm that felt far too possessive around her shoulders, striding toward the noise and laughter and lights of the party. Stacy had no option but to allow herself to be dragged along, wishing with all her heart that she wasn't going to be obliged to face the elegant crowd dressed as she was, but knowing there was no point in asking Hunter to spare her. She could tell by the fierce determination that radiated from him that he had set himself on this new path and was going to follow it to the end. Her wishes would matter little to him, if at all.

And it was every bit as bad as she had feared. It seemed

that every eye in the room turned in astonishment at the sight of the tall dark man sweeping into their midst with the ragtag urchin clamped to his side. Stacy had all she could do to keep from breaking away and fleeing into the night, assuming she could have escaped the iron grip that had shifted from her shoulders to her waist. Without pausing, Hunter swept the crowd, spotted Eric at the far end of the room, where he stood talking to a group of business associates, and paced purposefully in that direction. The smiling, drinking crowd seemed to part before the pair, and Stacy refused to allow her growing discomfort to show. Few of these people knew her and were probably awfully curious about all this.

"There you are, Eric," Hunter called out when he and Stacy were still several feet away. There was a ringing exuberance to his voice, which attracted the full attention of Eric's entire group. "Been looking for you. Why didn't you tell me Stacy was your sister? I found her scurrying about on the back patio awhile ago and couldn't believe my eyes!"

Stacy managed a faint, apologetic smile for her sophisticated, good-looking brother as his Rylan blue eyes focused in astonishment on his sister.

"Stacy! I didn't know you were coming to the party tonight," Eric said with a curious smile as he took in her disheveled appearance. "Why didn't you say something earlier when you were helping Leana with the flowers?"

"I, uh, didn't intend to come, Eric," Stacy began uncertainly, aware of Hunter's growing impatience to make his big announcement. "I left some of my tools behind and came back for them awhile ago—"

"When I found her skulking around the back entrance," Hunter chimed in, taking over the explanation effortlessly. "Imagine my surprise when I found out the

42

woman I've asked to marry me was related to you! I'd been assuming the coincidence of last names was just that; a coincidence." Hunter cast a deceptively fond glance down at Stacy, who firmly ignored it. She might have to play out this little scene, but she didn't intend to completely submerge her pride in the process! Out of the corner of her eye she caught sight of a surprised-looking Leana making her way through the crowd.

"I'm afraid I'm about two steps behind you," Eric exclaimed cheerfully, shaking his sandy-brown-haired head. "Care to backtrack and explain?" The question was directed at Hunter, but the suddenly searching blue gaze was on Stacy. "What's this about marriage?"

"Stacy's going to marry me," Hunter said with cool relish. "I finally got a yes out of her out there on the patio tonight. It's taken some doing, I can assure you!"

"I can imagine," Eric said quietly before turning to his circle of friends and politely excusing himself. "Come over here and tell me all about it. I must say, I'm a bit surprised. I had no idea you and Stacy even knew each other. Oh, hi, honey," Eric interrupted himself to greet his wife as she glided gracefully up to his side, her gaze on Hunter. "You'll never guess what's happened. Stacy's finally going to get married!"

Leana blinked, masking her astonishment almost at once, but Stacy sensed dismay. The poor girl really had already been weaving a few daydreams around Hunter!

"Congratulations," Leana murmured politely. "This is all rather unexpected, isn't it?" The long-lashed gaze went directly to Hunter, who appeared totally oblivious. What kind of a man, Stacy wondered in grim silence, could flirt with a woman one moment and spring a fiancée on her the next? Even though Leana certainly had no business getting remotely involved with Hunter Manning, Stacy had to admit her sister-in-law had some justification for resentment at this high-handed treatment.

"When did you two meet?" Eric asked curiously, looking first at one and then the other.

"Shortly after I moved into town a couple months ago," Hunter responded glibly. He knew practically nothing about her, Stacy thought, wondering how Hunter would bluff his way past all the probable questions. They hadn't even discussed a story that would cover all the little details. But Hunter was nothing if not fast on his feet, she acknowledged a moment later as he grinned cheerfully at her brother. "Look, I know you're all bursting with questions, and we'll give you all the answers in time. Just now, though, I feel like celebrating very privately. Would you two excuse us? I'd like to take Stacy out for a glass of champagne. I deserve it. You don't know how hard I had to work out there on the patio just now! We wanted you to know, though, before we left. So if you don't mind . . ." Hunter was already edging himself and Stacy away through the eager crowd.

"Hey, wait a minute," Eric called after them. "When's the wedding?"

"As soon as I can manage it. Probably the end of this week," Hunter told him bluntly with just the smallest hint of challenge. "It's going to be a very small business, I'm afraid. I'm not in the mood to wait for a major social event. We'll let you know the details. . . ." By now Hunter had his victim halfway out the front door. Stacy's last impression of the party was a ring of expectant, amused faces and her brother's bemused expression. There was one other image that stayed in her mind, she admitted as Hunter bundled her down the steps toward a sleek, expensive-looking foreign car parked at the curb, and that was the resentful, angry look on Leana's pretty face. She must be wondering why Stacy hadn't admitted knowing Hunter when she'd mentioned him while Stacy was arranging the flowers.

"Wait a minute," Stacy finally got out breathlessly, trying to dig in her heels prior to being ushered unceremoniously onto the rich leather seat of Hunter's car. "I've got my own transportation, and I'm not leaving it behind. I'll need it for work in the morning!"

"It's done," Hunter was saying, clearly not listening to her. There was a blaze of triumph in his face, which alarmed Stacy. It was a kind of savage satisfaction that made her wonder about the virtue of being single-minded. "It's done and there's no going back. Not after announcing it in front of all those people! The Rylans have lost a daughter. A fair exchange, wouldn't you agree? Sufficient payment for destroying my father. . . ."

Stacy was forced to fling out a hand and brace herself against the low-slung roof of the vehicle in order to prevent herself from being tossed absently into the front seat. Her resistance finally seemed to penetrate Hunter's consciousness.

"What's the matter with you?" he demanded, a quick frown darkening his face. He glared down at her as she gritted her teeth and refused to move. "Get into the car! Oh, for God's sake, I'm not going to hurt you, you little fool. But we do have some things to talk about, as I'm sure you can understand. . . ."

"You amaze me!" Stacy snapped flippantly, still not budging. "What could there possibly be for us to discuss? I thought you had everything completely settled. Why bother to talk over the details with me? I'm just the pawn in this stupid little game of yours!"

Hunter raised an eyebrow at that, giving her his full attention at last. "I appear to be gaining a somewhat sarcastic-tongued female," he remarked, ceasing his efforts to urge her into the car in favor of bending over her in a warning fashion. "It seems I'm going to have to instruct my 'pawn' in a few of the basic rules governing our relationship. There's no better time to begin than the present. Get into the car, Stacy Rylan, or I will put you there. Understood?"

Stacy held her ground, stubbornly refusing to budge. "You're the one who seems incapable of understanding things! All I want is to drive my own car home. I'll need it for work in the morning. Is that too much to ask? Good grief! If you're so anxious to talk to me, you can follow me home and we can talk there!"

There was a fractional hesitation on Hunter's part, and Stacy had the distinct impression he was seriously wondering whether he dared give in to her on even such a tiny matter.

"What's wrong?" she demanded bitterly. "Are you afraid I'll get the notion you're weak just because you display a bit of reasonableness?"

A very feral grin slashed across Hunter's hard face, and the gray eyes laughed wickedly down at her sober, rebellious expression. "The one thing I would never allow myself to be with a Rylan is weak," he assured her blandly. "And for your own sake, I trust you'll never make the mistake of confusing reasonableness with weakness! But, yes, I can be reasonable at times. Where is this precious vehicle of yours?" He glanced vaguely around at the cars parked along the curb.

"Over there." Stacy nodded her head toward the opposite curb.

"The panel van?" Hunter asked in surprise.

"Yes."

"Not quite what I would expect a spoiled daughter of

the Rylan clan to be driving," he commented, shutting the door to his own car and taking Stacy's arm in a forcible grip.

"But, then, you really don't know very much about me at all, do you?" Stacy retorted acidly as he started them across the street.

He laughed wickedly at that, his head tilting in the light of a streetlamp, causing the silver streak of hair to gleam for an instant. "I know enough, little Rylan. You've got the Rylan pride, and you're vulnerable. What more do I need to know?" There was a taunting, baiting quality in his words that made Stacy glance warily at him out of the corner of her eye.

"You think that's sufficient to want to marry me?" she said, coming to a halt on the driver's side of the van. She glared up at him in the pale light, her brows drawing together in a heavy frown.

"Quite sufficient, thank you," he mocked, reaching out to open the door behind her. "I'm sure it will be much more interesting using you to further my goals than it would have been using your sister-in-law. I should thank you for taking the initiative back there on the patio and introducing yourself! With you, at least, there will be some challenge involved in this affair!"

"Speaking of which," Stacy pounced, making another effort to mitigate her bargain, "why don't you reconsider my first offer? Surely the pretense of an affair with me will achieve your goal. I can't see that marrying me will accomplish much more."

"That's because you don't appreciate the subtle difference between an affair and marriage," he retorted silkily. "But I believe your father will! Only with marriage can I make you a Manning."

"You'd tie us both down like that just for the sake of

revenge?" she whispered helplessly, searching the hardness of his face and knowing she was arguing uselessly. Still, she had to try. Marriage to this man was a totally unnerving prospect.

"I'd tie *you* down," he corrected grimly, motioning her into the front seat of the small truck. "Now stop trying to make me change my mind. It won't do you any good, and the sooner you realize that, the better. Where do you live?" he added, closing the door behind her as she settled reluctantly into the seat. He spoke through the open window, his hand resting on the handle.

Stacy drew a resigned breath and told him. He nodded, stepping back.

"I'll follow you."

"We . . . we could finish discussing this in the morning. . . ." she suggested hopefully as she started the engine.

"We could, but we're not going to." He smiled laconically. "I believe in taking care of loose ends once a decision has been made. I'll see you in a few minutes. Oh, and, Stacy," he tacked on negligently, on the point of turning away to cross the street.

"Yes?" she muttered unhappily.

"You won't try anything foolish like attempting to lose me on the way home, will you? Even if you've given me the wrong address, I'll still find you. You would only succeed in postponing the inevitable for a very short time," he warned with a small smile full of lazy menace.

"You'd track me down like a gunfighter going after revenge, is that it?" Stacy mocked deliberately, putting the truck in gear.

"Not quite," he murmured, moving away. "More like a man going after his runaway woman! A much more violent matter, I can assure you."

Stacy didn't linger around to hear any more. She stepped on the gas, heading for the corner ahead.

Well, she'd really gotten herself into a mess this time, Stacy lectured herself as she drove across town to the small Mexican adobe-style house she was renting. Paul Rylan would undoubtedly find the whole situation marvelously entertaining. Would he understand at all why she had done it? Would he care? Neither her father nor her mother would probably have any idea of just how shaky her brother's marriage had become lately. And even if he were aware of it, the elder Rylan would be furious at the suggestion that his son couldn't handle business and personal matters simultaneously. After all, *he'd* never experienced any difficulty!

Stacy sighed again, glancing in the rearview mirror at the headlights following so closely behind. Her wayward imagination suggested it was like being followed home by the devil, and she felt a shiver course through her at the notion.

A pact with the devil. Wasn't that what she was making tonight? Stacy chewed reflectively on her lower lip, absently watching stoplights and traffic. She wished badly she'd had more opportunity to think back there on the patio. There must have been other ways of handling this strange, dark man with the silver in his black mane of hair. But he had controlled the situation from the moment Stacy had given him the option of using herself instead of Leana in his plot.

Eventually Stacy slowed down and stopped the truck in front of the neat little house set in a block of other neat little homes in the same style. Arched doorways, red tile roofs, and ornate iron grillwork were common themes throughout the neighborhood. The only things that distinguished Stacy's residence were the unusually attractive landscaping and the greenhouse in the backyard.

Hunter's sleek car purred gently to a halt behind the truck, and the piercing headlights were switched off as Stacy climbed out of her vehicle and jumped lightly to the pavement.

She turned to watch him opening his door and involuntarily remembered the legends that said the devil dealt very harshly with those who dared bargain with him.

CHAPTER THREE

"To what," Hunter inquired, sauntering forward to confront Stacy, "does the sign on the van refer?" He nodded toward the elaborate lettering on the side of the truck, which read, STACY'S NURSERY AND LANDSCAPING, INC.

"I should think it obvious," Stacy remarked sarcastically, moving toward her front door while she quickly went through the numerous keys on her ring. "I work for a living, Mr. Manning."

"You own a nursery?" he prodded, pacing along beside her like a dark shadow. She was aware of his enigmatic gaze on her profile as she opened the front door, but refused to glance up and meet it.

"Yes." She saw no reason to go into any detail about it. He'd find out all he needed to know about her soon enough, she decided grimly, leading the way into the small tiled foyer.

"Good Lord!" he muttered, nearly colliding with the huge fern hanging near the door. As he sidestepped it Hunter found himself perilously close to a low planter featuring an artistically arranged collection of cacti and succulents. "Do you run the business out of your home?" he growled, weaving his way with great care through the plant-choked foyer and into the small, cozy living room, where every window had been modified into a minigreen-house.

"No, my business is located a few miles from here in a commercial district where I have room for the plants and materials I stock, of course," she returned negligently, tossing her keys onto a small table and flinging herself down into a rattan chair, with its brilliant floral pattern cushion. She sat, feet stretched out in front of her and crossed at the ankles, her arms lying along the curve of the chair's sides, and watched him as he moved cautiously about the room. The flowers on her shirt clashed cheerfully with the chair.

"Somehow I never envisioned a Rylan working with his or her hands," Hunter remarked sardonically, going from one plant-filled window to the next. "Oh, a bit of skillful flower arranging now and then, perhaps, might be a suitable hobby, but I didn't expect anything on this scale!" He turned his head to glance at her sprawled figure. "Did Daddy set you up in business?" he asked, one brow arching with mockery.

"No!" Stacy blurted, and then quickly got herself back under control. She didn't want this man to know how disgusted her father had been when she'd announced her intention of choosing nursery work as a career. Knowing that might give Hunter a clue to the real relationship between father and daughter, and it was much too early for that. "I . . . established the business on my own," she finished quietly. "Rylans are quite capable of hard work. You of all people should know that!"

"And you're a Rylan right down to your toes, aren't you?" He nodded, prowling on to the next window. Before she could respond, he abruptly swung around and walked back across the room to take the chair opposite hers. Stacy was grateful for the low glass-topped table between them as Hunter leaned forward, his elbows on his knees, to fix her with an intent, determined look.

"A Rylan to your toes," he repeated softly, watching her frowning face. "Yes, it's going to be interesting transforming you into a Manning under your father's eyes."

"Do you keep your bargains, Hunter?" Stacy asked very quietly. "Will you really keep your claws off my brother and his wife if I marry you?"

"Yes, Stacy Rylan," he whispered in a dark, rough-textured voice full of meaning. "I keep my bargains. As long as you stay married to me, your brother and his wife are safe."

"Regardless of how satisfied or unsatisfied you may be with the pact afterward?" she pressed with a tiny hint of fierceness. "Regardless of the success of your revenge?"

"You have my word," he retorted with unconscious arrogance, and suddenly Stacy relaxed. Whatever else one might say about Hunter Manning, she was very certain he was a man whose word was his bond. If she went through with this deal, he would keep his side of it. But what would he do to her when he found out how poorly she would suit his goal of revenge?

Stacy sucked in her breath, her eyes never leaving his. "Won't you give me some idea of how long you intend to waste both our lives in this stupid venture?" she grated. "Six months? A year? What will it take to satisfy you?"

He smiled at that—a slashing, buccaneering grin that made her painfully aware of how much he intended to have her in his power. "You want to know the limit on your prison sentence?"

"It's customary!"

"What if I said I had no intention of ever dissolving the marriage?" he murmured evenly, the fog-colored eyes raking her bluntly.

"I wouldn't believe you," Stacy returned softly, certainly. "Sooner or later you'll realize how pointless all this really is. Or you'll meet someone and fall in love. One way or another, you'll want to be free of me."

"Or you'll want to be free of me?" he hazarded silkily. "What's the matter, Stacy, are you trying to figure out what to tell the current man in your life? Trying to decide how long to tell him to wait for you? If so, then I advise you to forget it. I'm not going to hold out the hope of a short-term arrangement that you can then use to talk another man into waiting. I've told you, you're going to become my woman; a Manning woman. There will be no other men!"

Stacy winced at the determination in his words but refused to let her fear and anger show outwardly. Instead, with a tremendous effort of will, she made herself shrug with deceptive casualness.

"Suit yourself," she stated coolly. "My own personal estimate is less than six months. Probably three or four at the most."

"Three or four months from now you will probably know better than to bring the subject up again!" he returned coldly. "Now, why don't you offer to make me some coffee like a good hostess and we'll get down to details?"

"Why should I bother being the gracious hostess?" she quipped. "If you want to talk, go ahead and talk." Stacy made no move to get out of her chair.

"Having made your deal, you're going to fight me every inch of the way, is that it?" Hunter asked almost humorously, sweeping her stubbornly relaxed figure for an instant before quite suddenly rising to his feet and circling the glass table to tower over her.

"We're not married yet," she breathed tightly, not liking the cool menace in those stormy eyes. She felt very uncomfortable with him so close.

"I'm not asking you to play wife, merely hostess." He smiled, reaching down to clamp hard fingers around her nearest wrist. "I really recommend that you don't try to defy me over every little thing, Stacy," he warned, yanking her lightly, effortlessly to her feet and holding her in front of him. "Save your strength for the important battles, or you'll be exhausted before the week is out!"

"Are you threatening me?" she hissed, trying unsuccessfully to remove her wrist from his grasp.

"Yes, I am." He nodded rather amiably. "Would you like to hear the gory details? I wouldn't want there to be any misunderstanding between us, not over such an important issue!"

"A cup of coffee?" she retaliated, refusing to back down. "You call that an important issue?"

"Small skirmishes add up to battles, and battles add up to wars," he noted. "I do not intend to make with my wife the mistakes your brother is making with his!"

"What are you talking about?" Stacy blazed furiously, wondering why he should be talking about Eric like that. It wasn't the first time this evening he had implied that her brother was failing to handle Leana properly.

Hunter lifted one shoulder offhandedly. "I've known your brother several weeks, and while it's obvious he has a head for business, he displays no sense at all in handling his wife. It was one of the things that made them both such a vulnerable target for me. I, however, do not intend to have the same sort of relationship with my wife," he remarked with such supreme male decisiveness that Stacy wanted to kick him. "My wife will know exactly where the lines are drawn and she will—" His words were cut off with appalling abruptness as Stacy, her temper surfacing with a vengeance, slapped him boldly across the face for the second time that evening. The blow was not a light one; she put her wiry strength into it.

"I don't want to hear any more of your Western macho theories on handling women," she stormed, dancing prudently out of reach as his grip on her wrist momentarily weakened. "As long as you're in my house, you will show some respect for your 'hostess,' and perhaps then she'll think about offering you a hot drink!"

She had stuck on the last sentence as it became clear Hunter was going to retaliate. She should never have resorted to striking him, Stacy realized nervously as she backed a little further out of reach. The promise of impending disaster in those storm-cloud eyes was unmistakable. The imprint of her hand darkened his cheek, and Stacy knew he was going to exact payment for the rash action. She prepared to run, perhaps into the bedroom or the kitchen, even though common sense told her it would be a totally useless effort. He would have her in less than a minute.

But in spite of the very plain warning in his eyes and the grim set of his mouth, Hunter made no move to come after her. For a long moment they simply stared at one another, he standing exactly where he had been, she clinging uncomfortably to the back of a chair as if to use the furniture as a shield.

"Come here, Stacy," he said at last, all soft menace and male purpose. His eyes held her in an inescapable mesh.

"What—what are you going to do?" she hazarded, feeling her fingers beginning to tremble on the back of the chair.

"Probably turn you over my knee and pound you so hard, you won't sit down for a week," he replied readily enough, still not moving.

"Hunter, no!" she squeaked involuntarily, some inner sense of justice telling her he had every right to do exactly as he said. Hadn't she slapped him twice tonight? Was it fair to operate under a code that said it was all right for a woman to hit a man and not expect retaliation in kind?

"Come here," he repeated in an even softer, infinitely more dangerous tone. "We might as well get this over with, don't you agree?" His hands rested on his hips, his feet slightly apart. The open neckline of his shirt and the slightly disordered dark hair combined with his stance to give him a thoroughly intimidating air. The streak of silver-white hair had fallen slightly forward, and Stacy's eyes went to it involuntarily for an instant before returning to the trap of his gaze.

"Hunter, you had that coming," she argued, refusing to obey him, although she could feel the bonds of his will reaching out to tug insistently. "You . . . you were man-handling me. . . ."

"I didn't slap you or hit you," he pointed out almost gently.

"Are you trying to tell me I actually succeeded in hurting you with that . . . that little slap?" she scoffed, raising her chin bravely.

"Yes," he said simply, lifting his fingers to the still-dark mark on his cheek. "It stings," he observed. "Badly."

Stacy bit her lip, feeling suddenly contrite in spite of the circumstances. "Does it?" she whispered in a small voice.

"I'm afraid so," he nodded. "Just because the Western macho type isn't supposed to show pain doesn't mean he doesn't feel it, you know."

Stacy swallowed, not seeing any convenient way out of the dilemma. "I'm—I'm sorry, Hunter," she tried uncertainly. "But you *did* provoke me."

"How much longer are you going to stall?" he asked mildly.

"I'm not stalling!" she gritted furiously.

"Yes, you are," he contradicted flatly. "It doesn't really matter, I suppose. I'm prepared to stand here all night, and we both know how it's going to end. Still, it is a definite waste of time to drag out the inevitable like this. . . ."

"Oh, go to hell!" Stacy blazed, frustrated anger lending her the courage she required to loosen her death grip on the chair and stride bravely across the room to come to a halt in front of him.

"I had the impression," he drawled, not touching her, although she stood only inches away, "that you think that's my native habitat, anyway!"

"Isn't it?" she challenged, using one hand to tuck a handful of unruly hair back behind her ear. She was shaking, but nothing on earth could have made her give him the satisfaction of her turning and trying to run. Her glittering green eyes met his unwaveringly as she waited for him to mete out the punishment.

"So you think of me as a devil, hmmm?" he mused, putting out a hand to catch her chin and hold her still while he studied her face. "Don't you know better, Stacy Rylan, than to make deals with the devil? He won't settle for less than your soul in exchange!"

"Why don't you just get it over with?" she rasped, feeling the tension between them as if it were an electrically charged force. Never had she been so acutely aware of a man or raw masculine power. This man and his power seemed to flow around her, enveloping her. Unwillingly she remembered his kiss on her brother's patio. He *was* a devil. He could make love to a woman or beat her without particularly caring which action he was involved in at any given time. She was a fool to have struck him.

"Surely," he began in a deep, silky voice, "after all that lecturing about right and wrong, which I was obliged to listen to at your brother's house, you're not going to pretend it's all right for you to hit me and get off scott free?"

"I—I really didn't mean to hurt you," she mumbled unevenly, knowing he was perfectly right. "I lost my temper. It happens sometimes," she concluded with a small gesture of resignation, her hand lifting in a short, flat arc and falling back to her side.

"Often?" he asked in such a strange tone that Stacy's eyes narrowed in sudden suspicion. Was he laughing at her?

"Not often." Not any more, she added mentally.

"That's fortunate for both of us, isn't it?" he remarked dryly.

"Hunter, if you're going to retaliate, I wish you'd go ahead and get it over with," Stacy muttered irritably, the dreadful anticipation worse, she knew, than the actual punishment. "Just remember I only hit you once!" she pointed out wryly.

There was an instant's pause and then, incredibly, Hunter was laughing. A deep, rich sound that, for the first time that evening, carried none of the deeply rooted anger she had been hearing in his voice. His hand fell away from her chin as he replanted it on his hip. The gray eyes were lit with a reluctant warmth that was totally unexpected.

"Going to try bargaining right down to the wire, aren't you?" He grinned appreciatively. "You know you're probably not going to get out of this unscathed, but you figure it's worth trying to temper the outcome a bit!" He shook his head ruefully. "You're a bold little thing, aren't you? Bold enough to deal with the devil. All right, Stacy Rylan, you've won yourself a reprieve. Consider it a wedding gift! Now, about my hot drink. . . ."

"I'll fix something for you," she agreed, drawing herself up proudly and turning on her heel to head for the kitchen. Not for the world would she let him see how terribly relieved she was. For a moment there she had been convinced he would carry out his threat. The humiliation of being hauled across his knee and spanked would have been unbearable, even if she had deserved it! She must be very careful around this man, she warned herself.

"What?" he demanded lazily, following her into the kitchen. "I'm going to get it without any more fuss?"

"If giving you something to drink will get you out of my house any more quickly, then far be it from me to hold up progress," Stacy grumbled, busying herself with the teapot and some cups and saucers. Her loosened hair fell slightly forward around her face as she worked, acting as a soft shield for her features.

"In a rush to get rid of your fiancé?" he inquired, lounging behind her in the open doorway and watching with sardonic interest as she went about the small task.

"We're not engaged," Stacy managed evenly.

"We have what I believe is known as an understanding," he contradicted firmly. "If you want an engagement ring to make it official, I imagine that could be arranged. . . ."

"I don't want your ring, thank you." Stacy eyed the teapot morosely, waiting impatiently for the first sign of boiling. Her tone was clipped and final.

"As you'll be wearing my wedding ring in a week, I don't see that it makes a hell of a lot of difference one way or the other." Stacy could sense the casual disinterest in him and wanted to scream. Didn't he have any compunction at all about what he was doing to her whole life? She had to take some evasive action, do something that would give her time to think of a solution to the mess. Her fingers closed tightly around the handle of the teapot as the water inside finally began to boil.

"Why must the wedding be so soon?" she asked, making every effort to sound remote and cool about it. She reached for the box of tea and measured it into the pot. "It seems to me that if you want the full effect on my father, you'd be inclined to invite him to the ceremony." If she could postpone the whole thing until next month when her father returned, there might be some hope. At least there would be time to do something; anything!

She turned around, the cups balanced on a tray, to find him smiling at her across the kitchen. It was his twisted, taunting smile, and her heart sank.

"Trying to buy yourself some time, Stacy?" he asked too gently, reaching out to take the tray from her numb fingers.

"I just don't see why we have to rush into this," she argued, trailing behind him as he carried the tray into the living room and set it down on the glass table. "I mean, I realize this is nothing more than a method of reaching your crazy goal, but you might take into consideration the fact that this wedding is going to turn my whole life upside down! Doesn't that bother you at all?" She dropped resentfully into her chair and automatically poured the tea.

"The notion of turning your life upside down pales into insignificance beside the impact I expect the wedding to have on *my* life," he told her dryly, picking up his cup.

"You expect your satisfaction at having had your revenge to compensate for any guilt you might feel about how you achieved your goal, is that it?" she snapped.

But he wasn't paying any attention to her. The fog gaze was focused on the contents of his cup. "What is this

61

stuff?" he demanded, not bothering to respond to her accusation. He tentatively stirred the pale liquid, sniffing suspiciously.

"It's tea," Stacy muttered, sipping her own delicately.

"It's not like any tea I've ever seen!" he shot back, lifting his eyes to meet hers. "What are you trying to do? Poison me?" he demanded.

"It's not a bad idea," she admitted. "I'll keep it in mind for the next time you bully me into fixing you something to drink! Unfortunately I didn't think of it this time around. What you've got there is an herb tea."

"Herb tea!" he growled. "What do I want with something made out of dried flowers? I asked for coffee," he reminded her bluntly. "I was willing to settle for real tea, but not this stuff!"

"It's too late at night for a caffeine drink," she said, sighing.

"If you're worried about how I'm going to sleep with all I've got on my conscience . . ." he began grimly.

"I'm not in the least concerned with your sleeping habits!" she retorted, irritated. "It seems fairly obvious that nothing's going to weigh on your conscience, since you haven't got one to begin with! I do not serve caffeine-based drinks in the evening to anyone, not even my worst enemy —a role for which you're well qualified! If you don't want that herb tea, go and find something else to drink. I think there's some fruit juice in the refrigerator!"

"Oh, my God," he groaned with a thoroughly disgusted look. "I'm marrying a health-food fanatic. I should have guessed when I saw you eating that apple instead of munching on some swiped potato chips at the party. A green-thumbed health-food fanatic!" He cast a baleful eye on the greenery surrounding him.

"It's not too late to change your mind about the wedding," Stacy reminded him with acid sweetness.

"Oh, no, you don't," he told her, the hard mouth quirking upward. "You're not getting out of this that easily. Tell me, though, how badly are you afflicted? Do you eat meat?" There was a purposeful gleam in the gray eyes as he sipped cautiously at his tea.

"I haven't touched meat for years," she told him with a sense of hauteur.

"I happen to love a good, rare steak," he said smoothly, watching her face.

"Then I trust you'll not expect me to cook it for you," she returned, just as smoothly.

"I do not intend to subsist on a diet of nuts and berries," he warned.

"It would probably be best if we each do our own cooking. You can hire someone to do yours if you don't like to do it yourself," Stacy suggested with a great show of unconcern.

"If you think I'm going to have a wife living under my roof and not avail myself of a few of the benefits of married life, you're crazy," he said purposefully.

"The easiest way for both of us to handle this disaster you choose to call a marriage would be to maintain a roommate relationship," Stacy pointed out, seeing a tiny opening. God! They were going to be totally incompatible. Couldn't he see that?

"Not a chance," he chuckled with a deliberately wicked look. "I'm going to make a wife out of you, Stacy Rylan. A Manning wife!" He took another sip from his tea, made a face, and set down the cup and saucer with an air of determination. "And since we're on the subject, we might as well clear up some of the details. I'll handle the wedding arrangements. As soon as I get a time and place I'll let you know so you can do whatever it is women have to do before weddings. . . ." He waved a vague hand to indicate the mysteries of trousseaux, dresses, and all the rest.

Stacy said nothing, privately thinking she wasn't about to invest time or money in preparing for this damn wedding. She might have committed herself to being the devil's bride, but that didn't mean she had to assist in the preparations. Her brows drew together in a resentful frown as she silently sipped her tea.

"I think it would be best to keep the details of our 'great romance' somewhat fuzzy as far as your brother is concerned. We'll just stick to the line that we met shortly after I arrived in Tucson and hadn't realized the connection with your brother. You'll want him and Leana at the wedding, I suppose?" Hunter broke off to confirm, black brow lifting questioningly.

"Not particularly."

He looked as if he were about to say something and then shrugged. "Suit yourself."

"Thank you," Stacy said caustically.

"I'll have a moving company handle the transfer of your things to my house this week. You're renting?"

"Yes."

"Then it should be simple enough," he nodded, as if planning a business arrangement. "Let me know if there's any money involved in breaking your lease. The furniture can go into storage until you get a chance to sell it."

Stacy said nothing, vowing she wouldn't lower herself so far as to ask this man for a dime. She continued to sit without commenting, quietly sipping her tea while he rattled off plans and instructions. He really did have a head for detail and planning, she admitted with an inner sigh. If she hadn't been so personally involved, she might have found it interesting listening to him put everything togeth-

64

er in one neat package. As it was, all she could think about was how little she mattered in this event, which was probably going to ruin a big chunk of her life. Just a pawn.

"I think that about wraps it up," Hunter said finally, draining the last of his tea and forgetting to grimace. "Unless you can think of anything I've overlooked?" he added with mocking politeness.

"I'm sure you'll take care of everything," Stacy said bitterly. "You've been working on the matter for fourteen years! I wonder if you'll get what you want out of this."

"You sound doubtful," he murmured, leaning back in his chair to study her intently.

"I am. I think you're going to wreak havoc with both our lives and discover afterward that it wasn't worth it," Stacy said with great feeling.

"Tell me about what I'm doing to your life, Stacy Rylan," he prodded in a low voice. "Is there a man who is about to have his heart broken when you tell him you're marrying me?"

"You mean is there a man who will sink to your level of operation and come looking for revenge? No. I don't know anyone who is that uncivilized," she whispered, thinking sadly of Gary Bowen. Gary, with whom she had so much in common. . . .

"Is that how you think of me?" Hunter half-smiled. "Uncivilized?"

"Yes," she hissed a little violently. "An uncivilized avenger who cares nothing about anyone else and whom I dearly hope will one day learn that you reap what you sow."

"Now, that," he said, grinning dangerously, "sounds as if you're hoping for a little revenge yourself!"

Stacy glared defensively, realizing she'd just fallen into a very neat trap. "If you've finished your planning session

and your tea, would you please leave?" she invited austere-
ly.

"Hardly a way to treat the man you're about to marry,"
he chided, not moving. "I think I'd like a clearer notion
of what wedded bliss entails," he went on thoughtfully.
"After all, this is going to be something new for me.
. . ."

"Really," Stacy demanded scornfully. "I would have
thought you'd found time to sample marriage sometime
during the past fourteen years."

"I've never had any desire to try it," he returned silkily.
"There's never been any need for it, you see."

"There's no need for it now," Stacy pounced with a
touch of hope. "It's still not too late to give up this whole
nutty idea and pretend it never happened."

"You don't know me very well yet, do you?" he mused,
his eyes flicking over her tense figure, taking in the
strained features, the dark, red-brown hair falling around
her shoulders, and the casual attire. "But you will, Stacy
Rylan," he added, his voice full of promise. "You will."

Suddenly he was on his feet, leaning down to lift her
lightly to hers, his hands closing firmly on her upper arms.
There was a new gleam in the cloud pools of his eyes, a
determined set to his mouth. Stacy didn't care for the
combination one bit.

"I think," he said softly, "that the easiest, surest way to
convince you there's no going back on our bargain is to
seal our pact tonight."

"What are you talking about?" Stacy managed, trying
desperately to stay calm beneath the passionate threat in
him. She knew what he meant, and the prospect was
outrageous. She was not his wife yet, and she certainly
wasn't in love with him. He had no right to expect her to

sleep with him tonight! But what did this man care about rights?

"I'm talking about removing all your false hopes of being able to talk me out of this marriage and all your incipient little schemes to bargain your way out. I want there to be no question in your mind, Stacy Rylan, that by the end of this week you will belong to me. I know of only one way to convince you. . . ." He made to pull her closer.

"No! Let me go!" Stacy snarled. "We're not married, Hunter, and I won't let you have everything your own way!" She began to struggle fiercely, planting her palms flat against his broad chest and pushing with all her might.

"Don't fight me, Stacy," he growled in a thick whisper. "You'll only hurt yourself!" He mastered her writhing efforts to be free, propelling her slender body tightly against his own hard length with an impact that left her breathless.

"I won't have it!" Stacy blazed, her temper blowing once more into full sail. "Do you hear me?"

"You don't have any choice," he told her bluntly, somehow managing to hold her forcefully without hurting her. He was right. She was hurting herself by fighting him, bruising herself against his toughness, but he inflicted no real damage on his own. Stacy felt like a small animal in a cage, hurtling painfully against the bars and gaining nothing.

"Damn it, you have no right . . . !" she panted, and then his mouth was crushing hers, giving no quarter in the battle for her inner warmth. He sought only some sign of surrender, and Stacy's instincts told her everything would go much easier for her if she gave it to him. But still she fought, unwilling to allow him total control of herself and her future.

"I've told you not to think too much about my rights," he reminded her, his mouth grating across the softness of her lips. "I'll take the ones I want!"

"Not with me, you won't!" she swore. "We may have a deal, but this wasn't part of it!" Stacy lashed out with her foot, aiming for his shin and connecting solidly. She heard his indrawn breath of pain and pushed savagely against his chest as his hold momentarily weakened. She was free!

"Why you little . . . !" He glared furiously at her as she backed rapidly away from him. "Don't you dare run away after that little stunt," he ordered, ignoring his bruised shin in favor of stalking her across the room.

"Leave me alone, Hunter, I'm warning you!" Stacy cried, edging toward the kitchen, her hand held out in front of her in a hopeless attempt to ward him off. His name certainly suited him admirably in that moment, she thought dismally. He was coming after her with all the deliberate, unswerving intent of a large cat closing in on its prey.

"There's no point in running," he told her coldly, matching each of her retreating steps with an advancing one of his own. "This time you're not getting off as easily as you did earlier. You're going to start learning what it means to be Mrs. Hunter Manning tonight!"

"This wasn't part of our deal!" she protested once more, almost at the back door now. Still, he made no sudden move to close the distance between them. It was as if he wanted her to suffer the distress of being stalked until there was no more room to run, no place to hide.

"When it comes to the fine print in our bargain," he informed her in a hard voice, "I'm the authority, not you!"

It was the steel in his words that finally sent Stacy over the edge of panic. With a small exclamation of fury and fear, she yanked open the kitchen door and ran down the steps into the backyard. The bulk of the greenhouse seemed to offer some shelter, and she intuitively raced to put it between herself and her tormentor. Then, in the darkness, she waited, her heart pounding. It wouldn't take him long to find her, she realized hopelessly. The yard simply wasn't that large, and he'd probably seen the direction in which she'd run anyway. . . .

But there was no sound, nothing to indicate his angry pursuit. In the tense silence Stacy tried to calm her breath so that she could listen more closely for the sound of his footsteps. Still nothing. The seconds stretched painfully into moments and the urge to sneak a glance back toward the house was overwhelming. Where was he?

It occurred quite suddenly to Stacy that perhaps he hadn't followed her after all. Perhaps he'd abandoned the chase in disgust. There had been no sound of a car being started, however, so she hadn't been lucky enough to have him leave altogether. That meant he was still somewhere around, but where?

Very cautiously, Stacy edged around the corner of the greenhouse. In the dim light spilling from the open kitchen door she could see nothing. A strange, fearful curiosity began to go to work in her head. She had assumed he would simply run her down, and she would be left to plead and argue and threaten uselessly. There was no movement from within the house, and Stacy finally summoned up her willpower. She certainly couldn't stand outside all night, and if he had meant to chase after her and drag her back to the house, he would have done so by now.

"Hunter?" she whispered breathlessly, taking one delicate step just inside the kitchen door. "Hunter, can't we talk about this? I'll give you my word not to back out of the marriage if you'll just—"

"If I'll just what, Stacy?" he asked mildly from directly behind her.

"Oh!" She spun around to face him. She had gone right past where he stood in the shadows of the porch! He was close enough to put his hands on her. With grim realization Stacy acknowledged that her recklessness and her impetuosity were both poor survival characteristics around a hunter who knew when to stalk his prey and when to outwait it.

"Go ahead," he drawled, his fog-shrouded gaze on her startled face. "Let's hear what new intricacies you're trying to weave into our deal."

What was the point? Stacy thought, resignation sweeping out all her other emotions as she stood looking up at his implacable face. Her wide green eyes were filled with reluctant acceptance of the bargain she had struck with the devil tonight, and she could tell by the glitter of male satisfaction in his narrowed gaze that Hunter saw her capitulation.

"It might be tricky getting a Rylan to carry out all the terms of a bargain that isn't particularly in her favor, but I'm going to do it. I swear it!" Hunter's words were uttered with such absolute determination and such a sense of overpowering inevitability that Stacy didn't even try to protest when he put out a hand, curled it around the nape of her neck, and lowered his head to take her lips.

CHAPTER FOUR

Stacy stood with a strange, totally artificial calm as Hunter's mouth invaded her own. She knew she should be reacting in some way, trying to talk him out of his intentions, but all the fight seemed to have temporarily gone out of her limbs. It was as if knowing he held all the aces in their uneven game had finally brought her the realization that it was useless to struggle anymore tonight. She stood passively, her eyes closed against the reality of what was happening, and waited.

"That's better," he ground out against the skin of her throat as his lips sought the small pulse there. "Your fate was sealed back there at your brother's house tonight. There's no point in struggling against it. Come and find out what it holds in store for you. . . ."

Stacy heard the soft, beguiling tone of his words and shivered with dismay. "Why do you waste words trying to coax me into giving you what you want?" she asked. "You've made it very clear that you're going to force yourself on me regardless of my wishes!"

"So now you're going to try the role of martyr?" he taunted lightly, not seeming particularly worried. His hands slowly tightened around her waist as he continued to explore the skin of her throat and shoulders with his lips. There was a slow, lazy, tantalizing aspect to his love-making that was disturbing something deep within Stacy.

"It doesn't suit you, Stacy," Hunter went on after a few seconds of deepening kisses at the corners of her lips. Kisses that urged and beckoned.

"Wh-what doesn't?" Stacy swallowed, feeling his hands pull loose her shirt from the waistband of her jeans. An instant later his fingers were on the warmth of her bare skin, sliding slowly upward toward her small breasts.

"The martyr role," he explained softly. "Deep down, you're a fighter, like me. And once you accept the fact that I'm bigger, stronger, and far more ruthless, we'll get along very well together!"

That was too much! "Not a chance!" she promised fiercely.

"See what I mean?" he murmured teasingly. "You'll never make it as a saint. But neither will I let you hurt yourself by continually fighting me. You're going to channel all that energy and spirit into a much more useful role. That of being my wife!"

"So that you can throw the fact in my father's face!" she charged bleakly, wondering yet again what Hunter would do when he realized how little impact that would have on Paul J. Rylan.

There was a fractional hesitation before Hunter bit out a soft, rasping "Yes!"

Instantly the cajoling, seductive element disappeared from his lovemaking. As if Stacy's accusation had made him realize there was little point in trying to coax her into a more passionate mood, Hunter, with a low growl compounded of desire and determination, bent and lifted her high into his arms.

"Put me down, damn it!" Stacy yelped as her senses spun momentarily with the unexpected change in position.

Without thinking about it, she closed the fingers of one hand into a small fist, raising it to use against his chest.

"Hit me once more tonight, Stacy Rylan, and I will really lose my temper," Hunter warned almost mildly, carrying her into the kitchen and on toward the living room.

Something in his voice, perhaps the very lack of obvious anger, stopped her. "Then put me down, and neither of us will be forced to go through any more scenes!" she ordered loftily, well aware she was in an exceptionally weak position from which to bargain. She glared furiously up into his determinedly set features. He smiled thinly.

"I wouldn't think of skipping this next little scene," he told her in deep, rough tones. He came to a halt beside the couch, patterned in huge yellow flowers, and dumped her unceremoniously onto it. "Don't move!" he grated as she tried at once to find her balance and get off the cushions. "Not one inch."

"What do you think you're doing?" she demanded as haughtily as she could with her hair in her eyes. He looked very large and forbidding as he stood beside the couch, examining his captive.

"I'm going to find out exactly what I'm gaining out of this deal besides a green-thumbed health-food nut!" He lowered himself beside her, and she tried to pull away, but there wasn't anywhere to move now.

"I'm not a nut!" she informed him stiffly, "and you're only going into this marriage for revenge, so you can't tell me you want anything . . . anything else!"

"But I do want something else. Something that will make the revenge complete. I want you!" Hunter reached out and took hold of her left wrist, chaining it deliberately as he leaned heavily across her other arm and upper body.

73

With his free hand he slowly, methodically began undoing the buttons of her shirt.

"Hunter, please!" Stacy begged, abandoning all hope of being able to hold him at bay with angry words. "Don't do this!"

The foggy pools of his eyes met hers, and she had the oddest sensation of being enveloped by the shifting, swirling currents there. His fingers were halfway through their task. She felt the slightly roughened tips straying inside the opening of her shirt, testing the softness of the skin of her breasts above the edge of her bra.

"Pleas?" he questioned, sounding vaguely interested. "No more orders or bargains?"

"Hunter," Stacy whispered desperately, her wide eyes making no effort to hide her anxiety. "I'm begging you to wait. At least give me a chance to know you and get accustomed to the idea of marrying you! Everything has happened so quickly tonight. I—I realize it's different for a man," she added, stumbling slightly over the words, "but I need time—"

"What more do you need to know about the devil?" Hunter asked with a mocking touch of whimsy as his fingers undid the last of the buttons and slowly, coolly pushed aside the material, exposing her breasts.

Stacy felt the angry blood rush into her cheeks and turned her face into the cushion of the couch. Her eyes squeezed shut on her fury and helplessness. He was right, she thought bitterly. What more did one need to know about the devil? And she had made her pact of her own free will, hadn't she? What right did she have to complain about her fate? She felt him touch her breast, slide beneath the lacy cup of the small bra, and then his fingers were gently circling, tugging, and teasing her nipple. Stacy sipped air on a tiny moan.

"Look at me, Stacy," he commanded in a low, husky murmur as he shifted to settle his full length along her trapped body. She could feel the steel in him, the smooth, muscled heaviness of his leanness as he crushed her softly into the couch.

"I said look at me," he repeated, as she refused to meet his eyes. He lifted his hand, the one he had been using to caress her breast, and firmly turned her taut face away from the poor protection of the flowered cushion.

Unwillingly Stacy looked up into the rugged, uncompromising face and swallowed dryly. In that moment it took all her courage simply not to cry. And Stacy hadn't cried for a very long time.

"I'm not doing this because of some uncontrollable lust I've conceived for a woman I've only known a couple of hours," he told her forcefully. "I'm doing it because my instincts tell me you're going to argue, bargain, and try to wriggle out of this marriage unless I make it very clear there's no going back."

"I'll honor my end of the deal!" she snapped, offended that he thought she would sink to his level of scheming.

"I'd prefer to make certain of it," he retorted grimly. "Besides," he taunted, thumbs toying with the corners of her mouth, "aren't you even mildly interested to see whether or not you can bear to have the devil in bed with you?"

"And if I can't bear it?" she challenged. "Will you call off our deal if it turns out I'm not capable of enjoying the act of love with a man who despises me and my whole family?"

Something hardened in the grayness of his eyes, and the line of his mouth tightened. "The bargain stands regardless of how miserable you choose to make your own life!"

"Because you'll do anything to complete your re-

75

venge?" she hissed, knowing it was useless to goad him. Nothing would make him change his mind.

"Because of that and the fact that once I've made a deal, I stick by it," he said arrogantly through tightly clamped teeth.

"Well so do I!" she stormed. Precious seconds ticked past.

"You want me to trust you?" he mused finally.

"Yes," she breathed. "Please." She could sense the thoughtful hesitation in him as if he were examining the idea from all sides.

"All right." He agreed so suddenly, she flinched. "Come to think of it, it might not be a bad idea if you learned to trust me, too. Give me a little on account tonight, Stacy Rylan, just to show your good will," he mocked, "and I'll give you my word not to make a Manning out of you until our wedding!"

"A little on account?" she queried suspiciously.

"Don't you trust me?" he asked, his mouth twisting cruelly.

Stacy stared at him for a timeless instant. The strange part was that she really did trust him. He was a hard, bitter, unforgiving man, but she somehow believed him when he said his word was his bond. He was too proud for it to be otherwise.

"A . . . a few kisses and that's all," she hedged carefully.

"That's my Stacy." He sighed, bending his head to set his mouth on hers. "Always trying to qualify the terms of the bargain!"

She stiffened beneath him as his mouth moved aggressively on hers in a sudden, sensuous assault. She felt him demand entry between her parted lips and grudgingly let him past the gate of her teeth into the warm, moist cave beyond. She had agreed to this, she reminded herself. A moment later she was aware of his masculine tremor of response and was startled to find herself reacting to it with a curious feminine satisfaction. Perhaps Hunter Manning wasn't as cool about all this as he seemed! For some strange reason the thought intrigued her. Instinctively she knew she was searching for a weakness in him.

"Touch me," he breathed, lifting his head to say the words warmly against her lips. He released her wrist and freed her other arm, at the same time settling himself more firmly against her. She could feel the rising heat of his thighs as he used his knee to force her legs apart and deepen the intimacy of their contact. Stacy felt his stirring maleness and shivered.

They were engaged in a battle of sorts, she realized vaguely, and their mutual anger seemed to feed another emotion. Perhaps it was the fact that passion was providing an outlet for her temper, Stacy thought wonderingly. It had never worked like that before, but then no man had ever infuriated her on such a fundamental level before, either.

Hesitantly at first and then with a curiosity she could not contain, Stacy touched him, her hands sliding down the length of his back and under the material of his shirt. She felt the warmth of his skin as her fingers made contact, and it seemed to send an electric shock through her whole body. His tongue flicked urgently into her mouth, and his hands slid around behind her to unfasten the hook of her bra.

Stacy had a fleeting thought that she ought to protest his going this far and then remembered his promise to cut the lovemaking short. She could trust him, and besides, there was a rising urgency in herself that no longer wished to be denied. It was as if her anger were transforming into passion.

"That's it, little Rylan witch," he growled from somewhere deep in his chest as he fought free of her mouth and went on to plunder and menace the vulnerable area behind her ear. "Touch the devil and see if you'll get burned, just as he's going to get singed in this red hair of yours!" One of his hands lifted to twist a section of the heavy, tangled mass around his fingers, and Stacy felt the sharp edge of his teeth close tantalizingly around her earlobe.

At the same moment she was aware of the sharp caress of his teeth, there came another, equally fiery summons on her breast as Hunter's fingers aroused it to a taut peak with a series of almost but not quite painful tugs.

The twin attack proved too much for Stacy's heightened, swirling senses. With a fierce, demanding little cry that seemed to come from the back of her throat, she arched against his hardness, her fingers kneading the muscles of his back with growing urgency.

Common sense and a remnant of her earlier pride tried to intervene, reminding her of how she had gotten into this situation, but there was a new element on the scene, an unfamiliar, totally unexpected, and altogether compelling desire that was sweeping through her. Stacy knew enough about herself to know that with the right man and in the right place, her nature was reassuringly warm and affectionate, but this was not the gentle, soft passion she had sensed in herself on previous occasions. And this was the wrong man and the wrong place!

"Hunter!" His name was a cry of longing and need torn from her throat as she began to writhe beneath him, her body demanding, pleading, insisting on more of him.

"Do you want me, witch?" he muttered fiercely, creating a trail of burning, stinging, exciting kisses down the length of her throat to the delicate curve of her breasts. "I want you," he said huskily when she moaned in response

78

to his blunt question. "I want you very, very badly. The devil in me needs to ride you until you cry out for mercy! Until you surrender completely . . . !"

His lips began a sensuous, teasing attack on her already hardened nipples, and Stacy thought she would die if she didn't have more of him. Desperately she fumbled with his shirt, almost ripping the buttons off in her passionate haste. In a moment she was twining her fingers into the curling hair of his chest, following the line of it to where it disappeared into the waistband of his slacks.

"I knew," he breathed, making her aware with his body of the pleasure he was finding at her probing touch. "I knew when you confronted me tonight on the patio, so determined and so brave, that there was a passion in you! A passion I'm going to own completely!"

She wanted to protest his masculine arrogance, cry out that he would never own her, but she was too deeply tangled up in the whirl of her needs and desires. All that mattered at the moment was getting closer to him. With every new touch, every new caress her body responded to him like a well-tuned instrument in the hands of a master, and she knew he was dangerously aware of the fact.

Later, she thought distantly, removing her hands from his chest to clench her fingers in the thick blackness of his hair, later she would find a way to undo the damage she was doing. But first she must find out where all this wild passion would lead. It was all so different. . . .

And then he was ceasing his assault, pulling back from the brink to which he had taken them. Hunter's large hands wrapped carefully, firmly around hers and trapped them quietly between their bodies.

"Hush, little witch," he soothed as she twisted restlessly beneath him. He used his legs to still her own and kept talking to her in a husky, soothing, crooning way until

Stacy, unable to move now, finally opened her eyes and stared up into the fog pools of her devil's gaze. The quick, shallow pants of her breathing slowed to a more normal pace as she continued to watch him.

He was smiling, she finally realized as reality swept back in with a terrifying rush. The desire in his eyes was fading rapidly to be replaced by pure masculine triumph, and Stacy knew with awful certainty that she had put a weapon in his hands tonight. A weapon he would not hesitate to use against her.

"I have never in my life been more tempted to break my word than I was tonight, Stacy Rylan," he told her in a slightly humorous, whimsical tone as he released her now-quiet hands and framed her face between strong fingers. "If it wasn't so important to teach you that I mean exactly what I say, I'm not sure I could have stopped when I did. But I can guarantee I won't be offering any more deals like that one! I'd never be able to survive them!"

Stacy was bitterly aware of a newfound respect for this man who had so easily overcome her pride and her anger to turn her into that passionate creature she had become in his arms. But it was not a respect born out of admiration for his skills as a lover or his restraint, rather it sprang from a new kind of fear. For some reason it had been easier to accept the idea of this marriage-for-revenge when she had been certain of her scorn for the one forcing it upon her. But the weakness she had discovered at his hands tonight threatened everything.

"You're so damn sure of yourself!" she got out between painfully clenched teeth as anger seeped into her blood-stream. "First Leana and now me! All you have to do is snap your fingers and the woman you wish to use is at your feet, is that it? You don't even lose any of your own self-control in the process, do you? A moment ago you cut off your own desire as if it were attached to an electric switch! It was more important to teach me a lesson on this particular occasion, so you simply turned everything off when you'd achieved your purpose!"

The touch of warmth and whimsy that had been lurking in his eyes disappeared at her bitter words to be replaced by steel, and the lines at the corners of his mouth tightened into their usual position.

"You think that's all there was to it?" he said, gritting his teeth.

"I *know* that's all there was to it! You proved it!"

"My God!" he snapped with patent disbelief. "I give you my word not to take you tonight, and what do I get when I keep it? Accusations of being some kind of robot! It must be true what they say about there being no pleasing a woman!"

"Why should you worry about pleasing me?" she flung back, knowing she should be backing down and quitting the field but unable to do it. "I'm only a tool you're planning to use against my father, remember?"

"I remember well enough!" he retorted with a touch of violence. "But the process of using you for that is also going to have the effect of turning you into my woman. And . . ." he went on caustically, "I have recently decided that one of the things I don't want from my woman is a lot of ranting and raving when she's lying in my arms! Now behave yourself, Stacy Rylan, or I will give you the beating I should have administered earlier this evening!"

Stacy glared mutely up into his angry, forbidding face and knew that this time he meant it. She had pushed a little too far and the only intelligent thing to do was back down. The knowledge was in her eyes.

"That's better," he noted coolly, sitting up beside her on the couch and fastening the buttons of his white shirt with

81

crisp, short-tempered movements. "I'm glad it's sinking in that I'm really not in a mood to soothe your ruffled feathers."

He finished buttoning the shirt and got to his feet to stuff the the ends of it into the waistband of his slacks. He turned his head to glance down at her where she lay on the couch, holding the edges of her own shirt together with fingers that shook slightly.

"I should have known making a Rylan witch into a Manning witch wasn't going to be all that easy," he growled, raking a hand through the tousled mass of his hair and forcing the silver streak back into place. "But I'll manage it," he tacked on laconically, starting for the door. He paused on the threshold, his fingers splayed along the edge of the jamb, and tossed her a warning look over his shoulder.

"I'll be in touch with you tomorrow, Stacy Rylan, and let you know exactly how much time you have before you become Stacy Manning!" With that he was gone, slamming her front door behind him with such force that the fern swung gently from the ceiling.

The phone call from Eric the next morning at work was not, Stacy told herself resentfully, the best possible way to have started the day. She was inspecting several boxes of seedlings that had recently been transplanted when the young clerk, Julia, called to her down a long row of hanging plants.

"Telephone, Stacy! Can you take it now, or shall I tell him to call back?"

Him? Stacy wondered quickly, her forehead knitting together in a frown. The last person she wanted to talk to at the moment was Hunter Manning!

"Who is it, Julia?" If it was Hunter, she was going to be too busy to answer!

There was a pause. "It's your brother, Eric!"

Stacy groaned and wiped the traces of compost off her hands. "I'll be right there!" Slowly she started up the aisle of plants, wondering how she was going to answer all her brother's questions.

"So you've finally gone and done it, Stacy," Eric noted with the easy familiarity of a brother who has long since accepted his sister's unpredictable ways. "To tell you the truth, Manning's the last person I would have envisioned you marrying, but you always have a way of going off on some unexpected tangent and surprising everyone!"

Stacy, who had never felt she was particularly strange or unpredictable, just different from the rest of the family, made some innocuous response while she absently pushed several straggling locks of hair back from her dirt-streaked face.

"I just got off the phone to Hunter a few minutes ago," Eric went on cheerfully. "He sounds like he's not wasting any time. I asked him if you two were going to wait until Mom and Dad got home, but he said no. I figured you'd probably be pretty swamped," Eric went on with a touch of caution in his words now, and Stacy waited to see what was coming, "so I went ahead and telegrammed the folks for you—"

"Eric!" Stacy quite suddenly panicked. "What did you tell them, for heaven's sake? I was going to wait until they got home to say anything . . . !"

"I figured you would." Eric sighed. "But they have a right to know, Stacy. You must see that. It would hardly be fair to spring it on them after all their friends and associates already knew!"

"I—I suppose you're right. Well, they'll probably shrug

their shoulders and tell each other it's about time. Did you . . . did you tell them who I was marrying?" she asked delicately, worriedly.

"I mentioned Manning's name, but I doubt if they'll recognize it. He's new to the area, after all," Eric told her offhandedly, apparently relieved she wasn't going to be upset over the fact that he'd notified their parents. Eric was very fond of Stacy, but he didn't understand her and he would have been the first to admit it.

Stacy winced and told herself there was nothing to be done about it now. She could only hope her father didn't respond to the telegram before the wedding, or that if he did, she would be able to intercept the response. If Hunter were to find out before the marriage that her father, as she suspected, would probably laugh about the whole matter, all her plans to rescue Eric would go down the drain. Her fingers tightened painfully on the telephone as she listened to her brother's comments and good wishes.

"I expect you know what you're doing," he rambled on affectionately. "Although, as usual, no one else does. Frankly, Manning strikes me as being a rather hard man; not the kind you generally go for. . . ." He waited invitingly for Stacy to explain herself.

"He's . . . he's somewhat different from the other men I've been seeing lately," Stacy admitted carefully, wondering how to respond. For once her brother was absolutely right! Hunter Manning was definitely not her sort of male! "Maybe that's his appeal," she went on flippantly. "He's not like the others. I—I have the feeling he's a good businessman, though," she added hopefully. Her brother respected good businessmen.

"Oh, he's that, all right," Eric agreed readily. "He's smart, and he's willing to take a few risks. He's also got a reputation for being a man of his word. People say he's tough but can be trusted. I know Leana certainly likes him."

Stacy bit her lip to keep from responding to that remark! But in some way it was almost reassuring to hear about Hunter's reputation. She was, in the end, going to have to rely on him keeping his promise about not bothering Eric and Leana. And she was going to have to pray he would stand by his word even when he discovered his scheme for revenge wasn't going to bring him the satisfaction he sought. What a risk she was taking, she thought dismally as she finished talking to her brother and hung up the phone. What a crazy, foolish risk! Her parents would probably say it was typical!

Stacy was helping a customer select a potted cactus and silently worrying about the telegram on its way to her father when the phone rang again and her name was called.

"It's Gary," Julia volunteered from behind the counter where several people were milling about, choosing bags of potting soil and small gardening tools.

"Tell him I'll call him back," Stacy replied, turning back to her customer.

"That's all right, go ahead and take the call," the lady she had been helping said quickly. "I've got the one I want. This barrel cactus will do nicely. Not much of a novelty out here in the desert, but I won't have to worry about constantly watering it the way I did that poor dieffenbachia I killed off last week!"

Stacy smiled involuntarily and went to take her call. She was not looking forward to this one bit. How did you tell a man you had been seeing quite frequently and whom you liked that you were marrying another man at the end of the week?

"Hi, Stacy," Gary's friendly voice came across the wire,

and she could picture him at the counter of his bookshop, leaning on the glass while he talked. His light brown hair, which he wore rather long, would be slightly unkempt, and his cheerful brown eyes would be idly watching the customers in the shop. "Thought I'd call and see what you were doing this evening."

Stacy took a deep breath. She would have to get the worst over with as quickly as possible, but she couldn't bring herself to do it on the phone!

"Gary," she began slowly, painfully, "is there any way you could meet me for lunch instead? There's something I need to discuss with you. Something important."

"Sure, I can arrange it. That little natural-food restaurant we found last week?" He sounded curious but not overly concerned.

"That would be fine. I'll meet you there at twelve," Stacy said quietly.

It was, Stacy thought sadly an hour later when she returned from the restaurant, a luncheon engagement she would have given a great deal to have avoided. She would remember for a long time the startled look on Gary's pleasant features as she faced him across a whole-grain sandwich piled high with sprouts and told him she was to be married.

He had been hurt at first and then angry, and Stacy couldn't blame him.

"Look, I know it's not as if we were involved in a grand, torrid love affair," Gary had snapped at one point. "But you could have at least mentioned there was someone else in the picture! I thought we—"

"Gary, until very, very recently there was no one else," Stacy said as gently as possible, her hand reaching across the table in a placating gesture that he shrugged off in irritation. "It's all happened very quickly. I've . . . I've told you as soon as I could, please believe me," she begged, green eyes beseeching. "It's a complicated story and one I really can't go into. You have every right to be upset. . . ."

And so it had gone on until Gary had cooled down, begrudgingly wished her luck, and walked out of the restaurant, leaving her with the bill and a growing, festering anger of her own with which to deal.

That anger, aimed at Hunter Manning and her own inability to think of a better way of handling the situation that he had created, increased with every block of flat, sprawling Tucson cityscape as she drove back to work after lunch.

The sight of Hunter's sleek, powerful sports car in the parking lot of her nursery did nothing to improve on Stacy's temper. With gritted teeth she slammed out of her own car and stalked into the shop.

He was there, talking to Julia over the counter. The attractive young brunette was laughing at something Hunter had just said, and Stacy realized he was smiling at the clerk in a pleasant, relaxed, quite charming manner. It was the sort of smile she never expected to seen turned toward herself. Not that she would have wanted him to smile at her like that, she thought belligerently as she made her way purposefully past a display of rakes and hoes to confront her visitor. The main thing on Stacy's mind at that moment was the unhappy scene she had just been forced to go through with Gary Bowen. Hunter Manning was completely responsible for that unpleasantness, she told herself grimly.

"What are you doing here?" she inquired with such an unexpected note of rudeness in her voice as she approached the pair at the counter that Julia blinked in astonishment. But Stacy's narrowed eyes were on Hunter, who had turned to glance at her the moment she spoke. The smile with which he had been favoring the clerk faded immediately as he took in the set expression of Stacy's features. The fog-colored gaze swept over her stained jeans and tulip-patterned shirt, coolly noted the uncertainly pinned knot of red-brown hair, which was in its usual midday disarray, and then came back to rest on her frowning features.

"I came to see you, naturally," Hunter told her in a dangerously soft voice, a voice that warned her that he didn't appreciate the rudeness or the frown. "I was going to take you to lunch, but Julia was just telling me you'd already gone."

Stacy glanced at her plain, functional little watch and shrugged. "It's after one o'clock. I usually eat at twelve."

"I'll remember that," he told her gently, too gently. He turned back to Julia, said something briefly in farewell, and then put a hard hand on Stacy's arm, guiding her firmly away from the counter and back into the large greenhouse that was attached to the shop. They had the place to themselves.

"Do you normally come back from lunch looking as if you would like to murder the nearest available person, or am I the only one lucky enough to be on the receiving end of all that fierceness?" he inquired laconically, drawing to a halt behind several stages of brilliant green philodendron and monstera plants. There was a hardness in his eyes and in his rugged face that he had not allowed Julia to see.

"Consider yourself favored," Stacy snapped, in no mood to humor him at that moment. "I've had a rough day."

"Who is he, Stacy?" The question was cold and full of the threat that she had so often glimpsed in his eyes. "Julia said you were meeting someone."

"A friend," she retorted, not pretending to misunderstand. "A very close friend."

The gray gaze slitted but otherwise Hunter's expression didn't change as he stood calmly taking in Stacy's barely muted defiance. He wore a lightweight, expensive-looking gray suit, and the almost-black hair with its eye-catching silver brand was neatly combed. Very much the successful young businessman, Stacy thought sullenly. What a fool he was to tie himself to her merely for the sake of revenge. He needed someone fashionable and socially active like . . . like Leana.

"This 'close friend.' You were telling him good-bye? Is that why you're back early and in a bad mood?" he prodded.

"It's none of your business!" she grumbled, annoyed.

"If you really believe that, you're in for a rude awakening," he retorted quietly. "You're not to see him alone again, Stacy, and that's final. Fortunately you had the sense to give him the news in a public restaurant, but all the same—"

"What do you mean by that?" she interrupted, furious with his calm assumption that he could order her life. "There was nothing 'fortunate' about it, I can assure you! I have the distinct feeling I'm in the process of ruining my whole life!"

"Don't be melodramatic," he cut in swiftly, frowning down at her. "I only meant I'm glad you were smart enough to meet him publicly and not in some private, isolated spot, such as his place or yours!"

"What's the difference? It wasn't any easier telling him at the restaurant than it would have been at his apartment!" she bit out, thinking of the trace of anger that had been in Gary's usually cheerful brown eyes.

"The difference is that you were far safer, of course, you

89

little fool," Hunter growled, his temper showing signs of fraying. "But it's over now. You've done your duty and told him—"

"Safer!" Stacy blazed. "What are you talking about? Gary would never have hurt me!" She looked up at him in a mixture of anger and exasperation. "What sort of people do you think I hang around with, anyway?"

The line of his mouth thinned, and she could see he was keeping a close check on his impatience. "Perhaps," he said evenly, "I'm making the mistake of attributing my own reactions to another man in the same position!"

"Hunter!" she gasped, astounded by the smoldering threat that seemed to radiate from him. "Are you implying you would—would—" She broke off, floundering for words.

"I'm saying, Stacy Rylan," he told her roughly, "that if you ever meet me casually for lunch someday and announce you're going off with another man, I'll use whatever force is necessary to change your mind!" He caught her by the shoulders and hauled her close. "You're going to belong to me, Rylan witch, and the devil never gives up his own!"

Stunned by the intensity of his words, Stacy was swept against him before she could protest, and his mouth came down on hers, marking her with a fiery brand of possession. Helpless to free herself, she submitted to the demanding, claiming embrace, knowing that Hunter Manning had set his seal on her. The devil's seal of ownership. And even as she wondered at the strange, cold fire in him, a part of her was stirring, questioning whether or not the chilling, potent flames in this man could be made to blaze with human heat.

CHAPTER FIVE

On the day of her marriage Stacy left for work at the usual time, stubbornly clinging to the familiar routine, although her state of nerves did not allow her to accomplish much, if anything, useful. And her nervousness, heightened as it was, could not be attributed solely to the wedding scheduled for that afternoon, although that prospect was awesome enough.

No, a portion of her tremulousness was the result of the night letter that had arrived the day before and that had been burning a hole in the back pocket of her jeans all day. She didn't even have to take it out to reread it; she'd memorized her father's brief message by heart. "Congratulations, Stacy," it read.

> "You always did insist on doing things your way. I wonder how long it will be before you realize what you've landed in this time. Look in the mirror, girl. He's not marrying you for your looks or your social polish, and I can guarantee he'll never be able to love a Rylan. But there's no point trying to argue you out of it, so I won't make the effort. You'll come to your senses in your own good time. Who knows? Manning may have taken on more than he realizes."

* * *

There had been no added note from her mother. Following a tradition that seemed to have been established in the early years of her parents' marriage, Paul J. spoke for both of them. Stacy sat back on her heels, studying some plants in a propagating case and bit her lip. The letter was not totally unexpected after being told by Eric that he'd sent the telegram. What was making Stacy so very nervous was wondering if Hunter had received one, too.

But if he had, she told herself reassuringly, she would have heard from him. He would have called off the marriage and raised hell with her for having tried to trick him. The whole point of the wedding was to enact a subtle revenge on her father, and once Hunter learned her father wasn't overly concerned with Stacy's erratic behavior, he would realize the pointlessness of attacking the older man through her. He might go back to his original plans.
. . .

She had seen very little of her intended groom during the past few days. After the first night, she had been prepared for him to lay siege to her physically in spite of his promise. The way he had kissed her the next day in the greenhouse had suggested he had no intention of letting her maintain any distance between them on that level. But Hunter had kept his word about not taking her to bed, and somehow that angered her further. He had been busy the short time since then. He had taken her out to dinner at a steak house and scoffed when she'd ordered a meatless pasta dish, insisted on her accompanying him to lunch another day, but there had been no move on his part to completely close the trap he was setting.

The sensation of a closing trap was an accurate description of how Stacy's senses perceived the impending marriage. She didn't like the poorly masked impatience with which Hunter awaited his wedding day. She knew he saw it as the beginning of the main thrust of his revenge. He made no secret of his anticipation, but he was content to let those around them think that his eagerness was for Stacy. He had kept his word thus far and not even hinted to Eric or Leana that there was something else behind his plans.

His kisses during the past few evenings had been hungry, demanding embraces, but he had not stayed long or pushed for her to come home with him. In fact, she had only been to the elegant Spanish-style house in the desert foothills overlooking the city on one occasion and that was to supervise the unloading of her belongings. She had taken a quick, nervous walk around the house with its floor-to-ceiling windows, curving arches, and decorative tiles and then fled. He hadn't pressed her to stay.

One of the things Stacy had delayed moving was the backyard greenhouse with its two hundred exotic orchid plants inside. The disassembly and reassembly of the small building would be a major project, and she thought she would handle it after the wedding. Later, when she was certain the marriage was going to go through. She wondered how Hunter would view the new addition to his cactus and rock landscape. There had been an unreadable expression on his face as he'd watched her hurry out of his house, and she still hadn't decided exactly what he'd been thinking. Then there were all her houseplants, which she hadn't yet talked herself into moving, either.

Stacy stood up, dusting off her hands, and glanced at her watch. The wedding was scheduled to take place in about an hour, and so far Hunter hadn't arrived in a fury to call it off. She could only assume her father hadn't called or sent a telegram to him, which meant her own poor plans were going to come off as arranged. Once married, Hunter was stuck with his bargain. He'd given his word. And strangely enough, even in a fit of his all too uncertain temper, she didn't see him going back on his agreement.

The roar of the normally well-mannered exotic car Hunter drove was the first indication of his mood when he braked to a loud halt in the nursery's parking lot half an hour later. Stacy was busy in the greenhouse, but she heard the threatening engine and her heart sank. It was almost time for the wedding. Had Hunter discovered the truth at this late juncture?

"Where is she?" she heard him demand of Julia, and the tone of his voice made Stacy swallow nervously. He was furious! Well, she couldn't very well run off and leave poor Julia to deal with him. Grimly Stacy wiped her palms on her jeans and started for the front shop.

He met her before she could get halfway down the long line of plants, his face full of the thunder of a desert storm, fiercely swirling clouds in the depths of his eyes. He was wearing a dark, beautifully tailored suit with the stark white of a silk shirt at collar and cuffs. The Italian leather of his shoes shone with the elegant gleam of lengthy polishing, and there was a flash of genuine gold from his cuff links. The heavy, dark mane of his hair, slashed with the silver streak, had been trimmed recently and carefully combed. He looked like the magnificent male animal he was, and Stacy wanted to run as fast and as far as possible in the opposite direction.

It was, she told herself as he slammed to a halt in front of her, only the perverse stubbornness that her family found incomprehensible that kept her from fleeing before the wrath in Hunter Manning's eyes. In that moment she was certain he must have heard from her father.

"What in hell," Hunter ground out in a voice of tempered steel, "do you think you're playing at, Stacy Rylan?"

Had she really expected to be able to put one over on the devil? Stacy stood very still, her slender body drawn up to her full five feet five inches, her knotted hair sitting like a slightly lopsided crown on top of her head. Only the green eyes gave any indication of her feelings, and they mirrored a strange combination of fear, anger, and defiance.

"You know, don't you?" she stated in a cool little voice that surprised her with its steadiness.

"Oh, yes," he growled, taking a step closer but still not touching her. Stacy had the feeling he was almost afraid to take hold of her for fear of losing his temper altogether. "I know! I should have known all along that a Rylan couldn't be trusted to go through with a bargain, any bargain, that wasn't one hundred percent in her favor! But it's not going to work, Stacy. You're one Rylan who's going to learn not to play games with a Manning! You're going to marry me today, and you're going to become a Manning tonight! You made the deal of your own free will, and I'm not letting you out of it!"

Stacy frowned. This wasn't the direction she had expected his attack to take when he discovered the truth. "I . . . I never had any intention of refusing to go through with the wedding," she said carefully.

"Then what are you doing in those damn jeans?" he roared. "And what are you doing covered in potting soil twenty minutes before you're supposed to be taking your vows?"

He didn't know! Stacy could hardly believe it. He was only upset because he thought she was trying to back out of the bargain!

"Hunter, I'm fully prepared to marry you," she assured

95

him quickly, relief temporarily chasing out her fear and anger. "Ask Julia. She's been waiting all morning to take over. It's the first time she's gotten to run the place by herself!"

He stared at her and then at her clothes. "I don't believe it," he muttered furiously.

"Didn't you get the note I left on my door?" she asked with concern. "It told you to come here. You must have seen it or you wouldn't be here."

"I saw it and I realized that you thought you'd be safer here when you tried to tell me you weren't going through with the marriage!" He was still accusing, but there was a new hint of uncertainty.

Stacy shook her head, not sure now whether to be relieved that he didn't yet know the truth or frightened that he still intended to marry her. She turned away to rinse her hands in a nearby faucet and wiped them on a towel as he watched in growing irritation.

"There," she said, tossing the towel aside. "I'm ready." Without waiting for any further comment from him, Stacy started toward the front of the shop. "We're off now, Julia. Are you sure you'll be all right? Don't forget to lock that back door in the greenhouse, will you?"

Julia, her eyes resting with deep feminine approval on Hunter as he slowly stalked behind Stacy, smiled reassuringly.

"Don't worry, Stacy, I'll take care of everything. . . ." She hesitated and then blurted, "I told you to buy a nice dress! I knew he wouldn't get married in *his* jeans! Oh, Stacy, this is your wedding day, for goodness' sake!"

Stacy blinked, startled at the younger girl's obvious distress. She glanced automatically down at her jeans and then, flushing slightly, tucked in her bright daisy-pat-

96

terned shirt. She was abruptly aware of Hunter standing behind her in all his sleek male finery.

"You, uh, knew Stacy intended to dress like this for her own wedding?" Hunter rasped softly to Julia, coming up behind his bride-to-be and putting a firm hand on her shoulder. A wave of embarrassment washed over Stacy as the other two flicked disapproving glances at her garments.

"Don't think I didn't try and talk her out of it, Mr. Manning." Julia smiled fondly at her red-faced boss. "But you know Stacy. She just doesn't care one bit about clothes, as long as she's got flowers on somewhere!"

"It would appear," Hunter drawled meaningfully, exerting pressure on Stacy's shoulder to aim her in the direction of the front door, "that I do not yet know Stacy as well as I should. But I plan to remedy that. Good-bye, Julia."

"Good-bye, you two, and—and good luck!" There was a small break in Julia's voice, and Stacy realized with disgust that the clerk was crying.

"I hope," Hunter grated beside his captured bride, "that the color flying in your cheeks right now is from pure, unadulterated shame and embarrassment!" He walked her briskly out to the waiting jungle cat of a car and, wrenching open the door, tossed her inside. "I cannot conceive of another woman on the face of this earth showing up for her wedding in her work clothes!" He slammed the door and rounded the front of the vehicle to slide into the driver's seat. He was still angry, Stacy realized nervously, but it was compounded mostly of annoyance. The blazing fury of a few moments ago was gone. His prize hadn't escaped him, after all.

"It's—it's not as if this were a—a regular sort of wedding," Stacy mumbled in a weak attempt at defending herself. "I saw no reason to make a production out of what is, essentially, a legal contract you're entering into for the sake of revenge!"

He threw a cold, foggy glance at her as he started the car with a small, violent motion. "This marriage is going to be very real, Stacy," he told her with poorly suppressed menace. "For your own sake, you'd better treat it that way!"

She sighed, sinking deeply into the leather seat and staring out the window at the Santa Catalina Mountains in the distance as he guided the car skillfully through Tucson traffic. A distant part of her mind insisted on noting that even when he was angry his driving remained cool and efficient. For some reason, that reminded her of the night he had swept her to a point of sensuous frenzy and then abruptly called everything to a halt. How could he exercise such self-control? When she lost her temper, things tended to get totally out of hand!

Stacy remained silent, and Hunter offered no further conversation until he pulled into the parking lot of a small church a few minutes later. That brought Stacy upright in her seat.

"I thought we were being married in an office downtown," she complained, green eyes narrowing as she noted a familiar car parked ahead of them. "You didn't tell me my brother and Leana were coming!"

"You displayed so little interest in the event, I decided not to consult you about the details," Hunter informed her, halting the car next to Eric's.

Leana, standing on the church steps, chatting with the minister, saw her first, and Stacy winced inwardly as her sister-in-law's eyes widened at the sight of her clothes. Then the lovely blue eyes went to Hunter, and Stacy knew that Leana was still building fantasies around the man.

The knowledge fortified her resolve. Eric's lovely wife would have been easy prey for Hunter Manning. A second later Eric turned and saw her, and his eyes, too, flickered disapprovingly over her clothes, and then a slow, resigned grin crossed his handsome face.

"Good old Stacy," he groaned affectionately, coming forward to drop a brotherly kiss on his sister's forehead. "Trust her to set a new style for brides this year!"

"Gracious, Stacy," Leana murmured, clearly a little shocked, although she had known her sister-in-law for several months now, "I would have been happy to help you select a dress more suitable for the occasion. Hunter looks fabulous, and you look—" Words failed her in that moment.

"She looks like Stacy," Hunter finished for her smoothly. "I imagine I should be grateful she at least arranged to take the rest of the day off work!" There was rueful acceptance in his voice of Stacy's unpredictability, although the hand under her arm gripped quite fiercely. Stacy had the uneasy impression he was almost defending her!

The wedding ceremony, held in a small chapel, went smoothly, almost too quickly, Stacy decided, considering the hidden agreements involved between the two parties. But the minister could hardly be expected to know what sort of bargain he was sealing, she told herself as the final words were said and Hunter turned to carry out the traditional kiss.

Instead of taking her gently in his arms, however, he planted a hand firmly on each side of her face, framing her searching green eyes and tremulous mouth.

"Hello, Stacy Manning," he whispered, and then he took her lips in a short, hard, decisive kiss that was over almost as soon as it had begun but which left her mouth stinging painfully.

Hunter brushed off Eric's offer to take the new couple out for dinner, saying that he wanted to be alone with his wife. There was such obvious male intent in the purposeful gray eyes that Eric laughed knowingly, collected Leana, and left. As they drove off, Leana's eyes rested lingeringly, wistfully on Hunter, who ignored her completely.

"So now you are legally a Manning," Hunter grated softly in Stacy's ear as he assisted her into the car a few moments later. She heard the satisfaction in his voice and shot him a swift sideways glance. He looked harshly pleased with his bargain.

"Just remember that you agreed to this as full payment for what you feel my family owes you," Stacy said quietly as he started the car and pulled out of the small church lot.

"And you keep in mind that you paid the price willingly," he snapped back roughly, his eyes on the traffic. "There will be no going back for either of us!"

Stacy affected a disinterested shrug, although her hands were tightly clenched in her lap. She had gotten this far, but what would happen when he finally discovered the truth? She would be the only one on whom he could vent his wrath, and she felt certain it would be terrible.

"I was going to take you out to dinner," he told her, "but I think we'll go on home instead. You're not dressed for the place I had in mind, and I'm certainly not dressed for your kind of restaurant! We'll stop at the store and you can buy some roots and berries or whatever it is you want for dinner."

"And you'll pick out a steak for yourself?" she retorted, becoming mildly irritated at the humorous way he viewed her diet.

"Exactly. Perhaps we'll be able to share the salad!"

"You don't think I could cook a meal you'd enjoy?" she

grumbled, vaguely pleased to have something else to talk about than the reasons for this marriage. Anything to take her mind off the forthcoming disaster!

"Not if that tea you served me the first night was any sample."

"Hardly a basis on which to judge a whole diet plan!"

He threw her a mocking, derisive glance. "You want to try cooking a meal I'll be willing to eat? Okay, I'll take you up on the challenge, but I'm going to buy the steak, anyway, just in case!"

They made an odd sight, Stacy thought later as she pushed a shopping cart through the aisles. The tall, dark, elegantly dressed man and the somewhat rumpled-looking young woman in jeans. Who would believe this was their wedding day? The unreality of the whole thing helped, she realized as she selected produce while Hunter watched critically. It was easier to keep from losing control and screaming to the world that it was all a huge mistake! Her mouth twisted wryly with her thoughts as she handed a plump tomato to Hunter, who dutifully bagged it.

"I think that about does it," she said reflectively, surveying the contents of the shopping cart.

"Except for my steak. I'll be right back!" Hunter disappeared up the aisle to return shortly, bearing his plastic-wrapped meat with a triumphant expression.

"You don't have to look as if you just went out and shot it yourself," Stacy told him indignantly.

One dark brow quirked upward sardonically as he dropped his package into the cart, but he said nothing, merely smiling wickedly.

The kitchen in Hunter's home proved something of a surprise. Stacy took a strange delight in all the beautiful new appliances and the endless counter space as she unpacked the shopping bags. The one time she had visited the house earlier in the week and made her hurried, dutiful inspection she hadn't really examined this room.

"What do you think?" Hunter asked quietly from behind her. He had left her to change his clothes while she unpacked, but now he leaned casually in the doorway, watching her. "Will you be able to cook your nuts and berries in this kitchen?"

She turned her head to make a flippant comment, but something in his eyes stopped her words. He was really asking how she liked her new home, Stacy realized with a start, and there was a totally unexpected vulnerability in those cloudy eyes. As if he would take the answer very personally.

"You have a beautiful home, Hunter," she told him a little stiffly, lowering her eyes to the lettuce she was cleaning. "And the kitchen is magnificent." Feeling a need to elaborate, she went on carefully, "I've never seen one so perfectly planned. Usually the top shelves are way out of reach for most women, and they almost never put real pantries in homes anymore!" Damn! Why was she bothering to be complimentary?

"And the rest of the house?" he prompted. "You took such a quick tour the other day, I was afraid you were turned off by the modern aspect. . . ."

Stacy glanced up, startled. "It doesn't strike me as being overly modern," she said quickly, frowning in thought. "Certainly not in a sterile way. Your architect kept the best of the Spanish look without making the place dark and heavy. And that little courtyard in the center is charming. I can see it now all planted with flowers and shrubs." A small, unconscious smile touched her lips as she considered what would grow best in the well-proportioned courtyard around which the rest of the house was built.

"No," she concluded with a decisive little nod as she went back to work on the lettuce. "Whoever designed the place did a fabulous job."

"Thank you," he murmured modestly.

Stacy swung around in astonishment and saw the self-deprecating grin.

"*You* designed it?" she asked in astonishment.

"Does that surprise you?" he inquired gently, folding his arms across his chest and continuing to lean negligently against the jamb. One brow was arched in a laconic way.

She thought about the name of his company, Manning Development Corporation. "I suppose I assumed you were strictly the business brains of the outfit," she confessed, gesturing vaguely with the paring knife in her hand. "I figured you bought and sold land and hired others to do the architecture and construction on it. . . ."

"I do." He smiled. "But in the early years I had to do a lot of my own design work until the company was established and growing. I'm not so involved in it anymore, naturally, but I still enjoy designing, and when I decided to build my own home, I wanted to do it all myself."

Stacy smiled involuntarily. "I know the feeling!"

"Of wanting to do things in your own way?" he said softly.

She nodded, thinking of how she had been forced to fight her family every inch of the way to achieve that goal. "Sometimes others are so certain they know what's best for you, and when you don't follow their wishes—" She broke off hurriedly. She mustn't say too much about that. He might realize . . . "Here," she said firmly, "finish washing the lettuce while I start the pasta." She thrust the head of lettuce into his hands and went to the cupboard to dig out a large bowl.

103

"I'm glad," Hunter stated some time later as he poured Stacy a second glass of the fine red wine he'd produced, "that your dietary restrictions don't extend to wine."

"Why should they?" she chuckled. "There's not an ounce of meat in a good glass of wine!" She lifted her eyes to meet his across the width of the hardwood dining table. "Speaking of which, aren't you going to admit you didn't even miss your bloody steak tonight?"

"The facts speak for themselves, don't they?" He smiled, forking up the last of his fettuccine. "I've had two complete helpings of everything! Mind you, I'm not about to forsake a lifetime of meat-eating, but with cooking like this, I might be persuaded to vary my habits from time to time. . . ."

He smiled into Stacy's eyes and she had the most peculiar impression of being on the verge of getting lost in the foggy mists of his gaze. It wasn't the first time she'd had the uneasy experience, but she was far from used to it. He looked as if he were about to say something else, something important, when the phone rang, breaking off the crucial moment as if it had been made of glass.

Even as he reached for the conveniently located dining room extension phone, Stacy felt herself growing cold. Intuition told her who would be on the other end of the line as clearly as if she could actually hear her father's deep, authoritative voice. She had a timeless instant of longing during which she would have paid any price, entered into any bargain, if it would have forestalled that call. There had been a strangely unexpected, cautious hope in the atmosphere between herself and Hunter this evening and now it was all about to be destroyed.

Well, she chided herself as Hunter spoke briefly with an overseas operator, what had she expected? This marriage was a bargain with the devil, and the devil was on the verge of discovering he had been cheated. She set her fork down with exaggerated care and watched as her husband's face slowly hardened into the arrogant, uncompromising lines she knew so thoroughly. He had realized who was calling.

"Hello, Rylan," Hunter said with a cold, fathomless quiet. "I've been expecting to hear from you." The gray gaze met Stacy's green one as Hunter listened to his father-in-law in silence. She saw the bleak, stirring storm clouds and knew whatever small hope had flickered in her this evening was well and truly being extinguished by the prospect of facing the full fury of her devil's thunder.

The conversation didn't last long. Hunter said very little, and Stacy knew he was exerting that disturbing self-control of his to its utmost. Only the deepening fog of his eyes and the taut lines of his face gave any indication of the force of his emotions. Stacy could do nothing but wait, her fingers twisted tightly together, green eyes full of wariness and determination. She had come this far and she would not run now. Besides, she told herself dismally, there wouldn't be much point. Hunter would not allow the one Rylan in his power to go free after this.

"Thank you," Hunter said at last into the phone with such icy contempt that Stacy swallowed in nervous response, "for your good wishes. I will convey them to my *wife.*" Stacy heard the emphatic stress on the last word and her fingers trembled ever so slightly. The phone was replaced in its cradle with far too much care. Hunter's eyes never left Stacy's bloodless face. He seemed as fascinated with her very still, very strained expression as she was with his cold and distant anger.

Unable to bear the awful silence and knowing she must make plain her own determination to force Hunter to stand by his bargain, Stacy spoke first.

"So now you know the truth," she said quietly, her chin lifting in unconscious defiance. "When you made the bargain with me, you attacked my father at one of his least vulnerable points."

"And you knew," Hunter returned with ominous restraint in every word, "when you agreed to the marriage, that Paul J. Rylan would quite cheerfully see his only daughter thrown to the wolf."

"It's—it's not that bad," Stacy defended herself. "He's actually paying me a compliment. He's learned over the years that I'm capable of taking care of myself, so he's going to let me do exactly that. The feeling is mutual. If you had said you were going after him directly, I would have stayed out of the battle. He's tough and he's smart."

"But when you realized I was going to attack him through Eric and Leana . . ." Hunter drawled, eyes narrowing slightly as he considered his tense wife.

"You had, with unerring instinct, found the family's weakest point. I couldn't talk you out of it, so there wasn't much else to do but try and convince you I represented an even more vulnerable point."

"Did you know your father would call tonight?" Hunter pushed his plate aside and leaned forward, his arms folded on the table. There was such frighteningly detached speculation in those fog-filled eyes that Stacy wanted to do anything, say anything, to push him over the edge of his self-control. It was her nature to want to get through the worst as quickly as possible. But Hunter would never allow that. Part of the punishment would be the painful buildup of tension and menace.

"I had a feeling he'd be in touch rather quickly, if only to let you know you'd failed," she admitted softly. "I had a night letter from him yesterday in which he did perform his parental duty and warn me not to have any illusions about the marriage."

Stacy's fingers untwisted long enough for her to dig the crumpled piece of paper out of her back pocket. She tossed it down on the table before Hunter and watched as he picked it up and read it. Her father's words burned through her mind once again. *Look in the mirror, girl. He's not marrying you for your looks or your social polish, and I can guarantee he'll never be able to love a Rylan. . . .*"

Hunter finished scanning the brief message, crumpled the letter in one fist, and looked up again, his expression coolly challenging. "But you, of course, had never had any illusions from the beginning."

"Hardly," she got out evenly. "What exactly did my father say?"

"In the briefest terms, he told me he was aware of the reason I'd married you. That he hadn't forgotten my 'dramatics' of fourteen years ago, although he'd expected something less primitive in retaliation than carrying off his daughter. But, he assured me, if I could tolerate a stubborn, ill-tempered, ungovernable woman who would make precisely the wrong sort of wife for a man in my position, I was welcome to her," Hunter told her succinctly. "He concluded by wishing me joy in my marriage and in my revenge, and he told me not to come whining to him like I did fourteen years ago when I want to get out of the mess. I got the impression," Hunter finished with a twist to the corner of his hard mouth, "that he thinks we deserve each other."

Stacy winced inwardly at the cruel words. She could almost hear her father saying them. But it was too late for both herself and Hunter, and she must make certain her husband understood.

"I told you not to expect any happiness from revenge," she whispered bravely, refusing to lower her eyes before the unfathomable pools of gray mist. "But you were so certain this was what you wanted. Well, you're stuck with your so-clever deal now, Hunter. You gave me your word that regardless of the success of your plans, you would consider the marriage full payment."

"What makes you think I'll feel obligated to honor my end of the bargain under the present circumstances?" he demanded remotely, one near-black brow lifting quellingly.

Stacy frowned slightly. "You promised," she reminded him.

"And you think that promise will bind me?" he prodded with lazy interest.

"Yes," she nodded resolutely. "I know you're furious, but you gave me your word. There's nothing you can do." She didn't for the life of her know what made her so certain of that, but she was.

"You're going to hold me to it?"

"Yes," she said again with fierce determination.

There was an instant's taut silence and then Hunter said in a tone of grim consideration, "Fourteen years ago I decided your father was a ruthless, scheming, arrogant bastard. But it wasn't until today that I realized he was a fool."

"What—what are you talking about?" Stacy was startled at the unexpected pronouncement.

"He's consigned to Hades the one member of the Rylan clan who shares his own arrogance and determination. Your mother, your sister-in-law, your brother, none of them would have been rash enough to try striking any kind of bargain with me the way you did that night on the patio. They would have turned the problem immediately over to Paul J. Rylan. Only someone with a full quota of Rylan audacity would challenge the devil. And the devil accepted the challenge."

Hunter got to his feet in a movement of coordinated power that made Stacy suddenly frightened in a way she had never been before. But she would not, could not run, so she did the only thing possible. She stood up to face her ominous-eyed husband, the width of the table between them.

For a long moment Hunter made no move to circle the obstacle. Instead he studied Stacy's slender, defiant form, his eyes sweeping over the slightly tousled red-brown hair clamped in a knot, the bright splash of color in her flower-patterned shirt, and the faded, tight-fitting jeans. Then his purposeful gaze settled on her taut features, and the green eyes clashed bravely with his own cloudy ones.

"Paul Rylan doesn't even have the sense to realize what he's lost," Hunter grated softly, watching intently as Stacy's hands flattened palms-down on the table in front of her as if she would brace herself. "But *I'm* aware of what I've stolen from the Rylans. The revenge has suddenly become a very subtle thing indeed."

"Are—are you going to tell my father what you had planned to do to my brother and Leana?" Stacy forced herself to ask.

"There's not much point. I doubt he'd believe me now. No, you chose to take it on yourself to pay for what the Rylans did to my family, and you say you're going to hold me to my word. Very well, I'm prepared to accept my stubborn, ill-tempered, and ungovernable witch bride as payment in full."

He was around the table in a few short strides, his hands reaching out to seize Stacy by the shoulder even as she involuntarily tried to back away. He drew her close, his fingers like iron on her shoulder. She looked up into his grimly intent, ruthless face and without much real hope tried one last bargain.

"Hunter, my father was right. You don't love me. Must we go through with this part of the marriage? Isn't it enough that you tied me to you legally? You'll have your revenge on me in a thousand little ways every day that I'm forced to stay with you. It's already begun. Marrying you deprived me of a relationship I was coming to value very highly. Can't you be satisfied with the havoc you've wreaked and will continue to wreak in my life?"

As she spoke the hand on her shoulder tightened and then moved up to circle the nape of her neck, and Hunter smiled, a very feral smile that gave Stacy the answer to her question. Without a word he lowered his head and took her lips in a slow, deliberate possession that reminded Stacy in no uncertain terms of whose brand she now wore.

"Any more additions, amendments, or modifications you'd care to try?" he growled in a low, deep, mocking voice as he lifted his mouth a few inches from her own and eyed the lips he had forced apart so easily. "Bargaining with you is always an interesting experience. One wonders when you'll finally realize you're stuck with the original terms!"

His coolly taunting expression struck sparks against the temper Stacy was so certain she had brought under control years ago but which had never been fully dormant. And the very fact that he could ignite it so easily was added fuel to the blaze. It wasn't fair that this man could govern his own emotions so well when she seemed to be at the mercy of hers!

"Sleeping with you was not part of the original terms!" she suddenly stormed, incensed by his manner. "I promised only to marry you, and I've done that! Don't accuse me of trying to modify or amend the deal, Hunter Manning! I've got my rights, too, and I won't be bullied by you just because I'm living with you! You're every bit as ruthless and arrogant and scheming as you say my father is, and I hope that someday you'll get what you deserve!"

"I think someday has arrived, little witch," Hunter bit out, bending down with unexpected swiftness to lift her high against his chest. "I am tied by the bonds of matrimony and my own word to a woman who is independent, bad-tempered, obstinate, and, until recently, uncontrollable." He started down the hall, a furious Stacy in his arms. "Fortunately," he added with resolution, "I can do something about that last problem!"

"I won't have you threatening me," she hissed fiercely, afraid to struggle too violently in case he simply dropped her to the floor. It was strangely unnerving to be carried in a man's arms. It gave a woman a frightening sense of powerlessness, she was discovering. And when the destination was the man's bedroom, as Hunter's goal obviously was, the sensation was almost overwhelming.

"I'm not threatening you, witch," he retorted, carrying her past the row of windows that looked out on the interior courtyard. "I'm making you a promise!" He turned at the darkened entrance to the master bedroom, a room Stacy had glimpsed only fleetingly.

He set her on her feet, a firm hand on her wrist as he reached out to turn on the bedside lamp, illuminating the solid, massive furniture around her. Stacy blinked as she regained her balance, glancing automatically about for some avenue of escape. But everything that met her eyes seemed to reinforce the feeling of being trapped. The room reflected the uncompromising masculinity of her husband, with its wide, low bed, brass-trimmed chest of drawers, and old, valuable Navaho rugs. One windowed wall looked out on the privacy of the courtyard, giving the impression of being partially outdoors. In the glow of the lamp, Hunter viewed his captive, his fingers never releasing her wrist.

With a rising sense of desperation, Stacy glared up at him, her wrist becoming a little raw as she pulled and twisted it, trying to free herself.

"Hunter, I won't be forced into this! You have no right . . ."

"I've warned you before about that subject." He half-smiled, tightening his fingers on the small bones of her wrist so that she could no longer even struggle. When she glanced angrily down at his grip, he followed the direction of her focus and said softly, "I won't let you bruise yourself against me, Stacy Manning. You belong to me now, and the devil takes care of his own."

CHAPTER SIX

Stacy's glittering green eyes lifted from the sight of her manacled wrist and collided with the implacable gaze of her husband.

"Well?" he invited with gentle menace, "are you going to try slapping me again?"

"You'd like that, wouldn't you?" she snapped, reading the hopelessness of her situation in his eyes and refusing to surrender. "You'd welcome an excuse for using your brute strength against me!"

He shrugged. "Not particularly. There are other things I'd rather do with you at the moment. But if we have to go through that lesson first, I'm willing." His mouth twisted in a small smile as he studied her mutinous face. "Do you really want to fight me, little witch? Remember how it was the first night when we made our bargain? And what about the kisses we've shared since then. . . ."

He lifted his free hand and thrust his fingers through the heaviness of her hair, sending the clip flying into the darkness beyond the lamp and watching with male satisfaction as her thick hair tumbled down around her shoulders.

"Don't . . . !" Stacy gasped as he calmly went to work on the buttons of her shirt, but with only one hand to defend herself, she couldn't stop him. Desperately she clutched at his wrist, trying to pull it away, but he ignored the small effort. "I won't . . . I won't go to bed with a man who can turn his emotions on like a robot! The only reason you want me tonight is to consolidate your revenge! You don't feel any real passion or—or love, or—" She stumbled over the words, a furious red rising into her cheeks.

"So that's what this is all about," he whispered. "You haven't forgiven me for that first night when I walked out after having given you my word not to take you. And you must be holding this whole week of rather restrained lovemaking against me, too. But there was a reason for my self-control, little witch," he explained, finishing his work on the buttons and using his hand to cup her chin. "I couldn't risk having you panic and refuse to go through with the wedding, could I? After all, until your father's phone call tonight, I was convinced marrying you was the best way to achieve my goal."

"That's exactly what I mean!" Stacy wailed helplessly. "All you can think about is your damn revenge!" Didn't he understand? Didn't he have any compassion for her feelings in the matter? What woman wanted the humiliation of surrendering completely in the arms of a man who wouldn't allow himself to lose his own control in the process? Whose passion was merely another weapon for achieving his goal of revenge?

"Make me think of something else, then, witch," he challenged suddenly, releasing her wrist long enough to push the daisy-splattered shirt off her shoulders. Before she could take advantage of the loosened grip, however, he had an arm clamped firmly around her waist, holding her still while he unclasped the honey-colored bra. An instant later the scrap of material fell to the floor, and Stacy, naked from the waist up, knew there was no point in pleading with him any longer. With a small, hopeless cry she turned her face into his shoulder, unable to meet his gaze while she stood before him like this.

He allowed her to hide her eyes while his hand slipped warmly up from the skin of her narrow waist to palm the nipple of one breast. She heard his sharply indrawn breath, and then his lips were in her hair, inhaling the fresh, clean scent of it while his hand explored the shape of her softness.

"Small and delicate and so tempting," he murmured, his fingers tugging at the nipple gently at first and then with increasing demand. Stacy shivered as the tip of her breast hardened in response to his touch. Memories of her passion once before in his arms came flooding back, weakening her resolve to be free of him. Instead a new kind of desire was growing in her. A desire to make her devil of a husband lose his self-mastery in the one way a woman should be able to manage. Could *she* manage it?

If only, Stacy thought, aware of the uncontrollable little tremor that rippled through her at his touch, she could defeat him at his own game. Make him know a degree of passion so intense that, at least for the time he lay in her arms, he forgot about his revenge and everything else in the world. It was an intoxicating idea, the appeal of which grew with every passing second. She could not hope to fight this man with the inadequate strength of her body, nor could she win by pitting her willpower alone against his. But Stacy knew how to fight to get what she wanted. Hadn't she been doing it in one way or another all her life? There must be a way to get what she wanted from Hunter Manning.

Stacy felt the compulsion of his arm against her lower back, propelling her thighs against him. His body seemed to radiate a sensuous heat that carried the scent of his maleness to her sensitive nostrils. As if he were one of her prize orchids, she breathed in the aroma of him, finding it an enticing and provocative combination of after-shave, masculine sweat, and the earthy smell of the desert at night.

Slowly, inevitably, Stacy wound her arms around his neck, her fingers finding and exploring the thick darkness of his hair at the nape. Unable to help herself, she responded to the impetus of his arm and arched against him, aware of the texture of his shirt against her breasts.

"That's it, little witch," he growled, his voice carrying a new huskiness. "I want to know the passion in you in a way no other man will ever be allowed to know now that you belong to me!" His fingers traced the line of her spine down to the waistband of her jeans, sliding inside and around to the clasp in front.

"Hunter . . . do you want me, really want me?" Stacy heard herself ask thickly, her eyes closing as she felt him undo the jeans and begin to slide them over the curve of her hip.

"Oh, yes, my sweet, green-eyed witch," he vowed as he stripped the denim from her. "I want you. I'm more than willing to consummate our bargain tonight. You're woman enough to recognize the signs, surely?" He half-chuckled, leaning down to pull back the covers of the wide bed. A second later he had picked her up and set her in the middle of it, where she lay in only her briefs. He stood looking down at her for a moment, his eyes traveling from the dark fire of her hair across the pillow, across the small peaks of her breasts, and then coming to rest on her one, remaining garment. A slow, slashing smile crossed his face.

"Well, I'll be damned. You really do like flowers, don't you?" He reached down to run a finger just inside the elastic waist of her prim cotton underpants with their bright flower design.

Stacy, abruptly resentful of his gentle mockery, scooted across the bed, just out of reach. "Are you going to laugh at me on top of everything else?" she asked in a flat little voice, her eyes accusing.

"No, flower lady," he soothed, his fingers at work on the fastenings of his own clothes. "I'm going to enjoy you, not laugh at you. There's a difference." He dropped his shirt across a nearby chair, and Stacy blinked at the hard, lean length of him as he quickly stepped out of his remaining clothes.

There was an overpowering masculinity about him that reached out to something deep and hidden in Stacy, something she couldn't fight. Instead it made her want to grasp hold of its essence and draw it to herself. In the confusion of emotions flooding her at that moment, she couldn't put a name to the attraction Hunter held for her. She only knew it was not a mere physical thing. It was far more potent, bound up as it was with the force of his will, his determination to make his own rules, and Stacy's instinctive, inexplicable knowledge that, once committed, Hunter could be trusted to the ends of the earth. As she lay there watching him undress in the lamplight, Stacy suddenly knew that she wanted him to be totally committed to her. In that there lay a measure of safety.

Before she could analyze and assess the meaning of her feelings and desires, Hunter was beside her on the bed, putting out a hand to pull her tightly against his strength. She felt his legs tangle with her own, trapping them gently, firmly, totally. The crisp, curling hair of his chest teased her breasts as he moved sensuously against her. He was rather like a large cat luxuriating near the warmth of an open hearth, she thought vaguely, unable to resist first a

117

hesitant touch and then a small, stroking exploration of the line of his lean waist and narrow hip.

"You're going to be my own private flower garden, honey," he whispered deeply, bending over her to nibble carefully at the tip of her ear. "I'm going to be able to wander in any time and gather a handful of blossoms. Blossoms that no other man can touch now that you're mine. Will you like switching roles and becoming the garden instead of the gardener?" he added with a strange whimsy as his hands trailed possessively, urgently across her breasts and down to the briefs he had mocked a moment earlier.

"Do you think," she whispered in a small, pleading little voice as his fingers slipped under the edge of her last piece of clothing and removed it, "that you really want the responsibility of a garden, Hunter?" She lifted her head higher on the pillow, enough to meet the gray evening fog of his gaze.

"Are you afraid I won't know how to tend my flowers?" he murmured, putting his lips on her throat, tracking lazily, languidly down to the small bones in the hollow of her shoulder. "Have no fear of that. I'll admit this is the first time I've ever owned a garden, but I know what I want out of it, and I'll do all the necessary labor involved." He gave a soft, husky laugh that originated deep in his chest, and then his mouth was tracing the path of his fingers down to the curve of her small breasts.

Stacy sucked in her breath as she felt his fingers move in a randomly exciting pattern against the skin of her stomach. Involuntarily she shivered, seeking more of his warmth.

"Gardens . . ." she began a little desperately, her face buried in the heat of his chest. "Gardens can be very demanding. . . ." Her fingers flexed into his hard muscled

118

back as the pattern he was drawing on her stomach was extended to the inner softness of her thigh.

"So can gardeners," he told her thickly, letting her know the rising masculine desire in his hard body. She felt a tremor go through him as she raked her fingers gently down the length of his back to the base of his spine. He shifted, sprawling more heavily against her, and his weight crowded her deeply into the bedclothes beneath him.

"Tell me," he invited in a low growl, "what my garden would have of me!"

Stacy closed her eyes against the heavy currents of passion beginning to wash through her, and her answer came interspersed with a quickening series of small pants.

"Gardens need someone who understands them, cares for them, someone who—who needs them in return—" Stacy gasped as Hunter's hand prowled closer to the ultrasensitive warm core of her.

"And this gardener wants a patch of flowers that looks toward him for its strength rather than toward the sun or anything else," Hunter said with sudden, quiet fierceness, his fingers growing bolder and more aggressive by the second. The lazy, languid approach he had been taking was fading rapidly as he felt her rising response.

"Oh, Hunter," Stacy got out in a tight, quick-breathed voice as he began to probe the most intimate places of her body, seeking, teasing, coaxing until she began to twist and writhe beneath him. "Yes," she whispered helplessly, succumbing to the waves of sensation he was creating. Her arms wrapped around him, clutching him more closely to her arching body, and she began to plant tiny, demanding little kisses against the tanned column of his throat.

"Tell me you want me, flower witch," he grated against the silky smoothness of her skin. She heard the demand in his words and wondered briefly at it. Wasn't it obvious that she was becoming that strange creature he created when he held her like this? He must be aware of her desire!

"Tell me," he insisted in a voice that was turning raspy. It slithered along her nerve endings, heightening his demand for a response.

"I want you, Hunter," she heard herself say almost harshly. "You must know that!"

"I want you to know it," he retorted with a new passion. "Know it and admit it to me and to yourself!"

He would make her totally his, she realized in some distant part of her mind. Totally a Manning bride. Tonight he sought to complete his revenge, limited though it had become. He was using the lack of self-control she experienced in his arms to consolidate his hold on her. After tonight there would be no question of whose woman she was. In the most primitive sense of the word, she would belong to Hunter Manning.

There was nothing she could do about it, Stacy knew. She could not deny the power of him. Her only salvation lay in showing him that the sort of bonds he sought to impose tied both the bound one and the one who held the chains. Hunter might think to possess her, but she would do her best to teach her arrogant, coldly passionate husband that there was a price for such possession. The possessor risked becoming possessed. Hunter would learn what it meant to have a wife!

With a pulsating need Stacy responded completely to the overwhelming, mastering, reckless passion Hunter elicited. It was strange to find her body reacting like this, as if it had long sought the challenge this man presented. She clung to him, imposing the countless demands of a woman in the arms of her lover, demands women had instinctively imposed since the beginning of time. And men like Hunter, their masculinity so primitive and potent as to make them seem almost out of place in the twentieth century, took an arrogant satisfaction in fulfilling those feminine commands, not realizing that each time they did so they dug themselves deeper and deeper into the quicksand magic of a witch. There would come a point, Stacy knew with sudden intuition, when Hunter would be caught, unable and unwilling to free himself. Pushed beyond some important point, Hunter would become a victim of the desire he had deliberately created in her.

"Ah, sweet, green-eyed witch," he said, his own breath coming now in shorter, more violent pants, his body trembling slightly each time she shivered, although he still seemed in control. "You will flower only in my arms! You will need only me to make you feel like this!"

"Yes, Hunter," Stacy responded, aware that he was beginning to demand access for his legs between hers. She felt the first, tentative insistence of his knee as it sought to part her limbs and open her up completely to his invasion. She also felt the momentary astonishment and arrogant, male disbelief when she refused to cooperate. And the witch in her laughed silently.

He waited a moment longer, talking to her gently, beguilingly, his hands eliciting more and more of the telltale shivers that now racked her body almost constantly.

"Come, little garden," he whispered deeply, coaxingly. "Open the gate and let me collect some blossoms. I know you want your gardener inside. . . ." Once again his knee pressed insistently, seeking to part her legs, and once more Stacy, though she arched passionately against him, refused admittance.

"Why do you resist, flower witch?" he murmured, stroking her inner thigh with encouraging, arousing fingers. "You want this as much as I. See how heated and moist and welcoming you are. . . ."

"How much do you want it, Hunter?" she breathed tantalizingly, her green eyes glittering up into his as he lifted his head to look down into her love-softened face. She saw the storm of his male need swirling in the depths of his gray eyes, which collided with hers, and half-smiled, putting up a hand to toy with the silver in his dark hair.

"By God, witch," he grated, clearly astounded. "Would you play games with me tonight?" And suddenly the masculine passion in his eyes hardened into something beyond the normal level of desire. Stacy saw it and wondered what she had unleashed. But it was too late to change her mind about how to deal with Hunter Manning.

In a flash she felt her wrists caught and pinned on either side of her head. With a low, fierce growl, Hunter settled fully on top of her soft, slender body, not asking for admittance between her legs this time but forcing them inexorably apart with his knee.

"Do you want to try another bargain, is that it, witch?" he snarled softly. "Did you really think I would let you do that to me in bed? You're mine, Stacy, and I'll take what is mine. There will be no bargaining between us in bed!"

Still anchoring her wrists, Hunter lowered his head to Stacy's parted lips, and in the instant before he took them she saw the deep mists of his eyes flickering with silver flames that trapped her once and for all. His mouth closed over hers at the same instant that he moved strongly against her, making them one in a thrilling, overpowering union.

Stacy surrendered completely. Not even the ancient, aroused witchcraft in her could fight him or taunt him or bargain with him now. She was his and in that moment of being claimed, body and soul, there was no room for pretense or games. She knew with every nerve in her that

122

Hunter was aware of the completeness of the capitulation, but she no longer cared. The only important thing in the world was to respond to the forceful, dizzying rhythm he established. The small, female sounds that came from the back of her throat seemed to goad him into taking her higher and higher in a spiral of sensation. The spiral tightened, intensified, made her senses swim until she lost all awareness of anything else in the universe but the world she shared with Hunter. And then, with a last, incredibly arousing movement, it all dissolved in a blazing, shimmering burst of light and heat.

A long while later Stacy slowly opened her eyes, aware of the weight of her husband as he still sprawled partially across her, his head resting heavily beside her on the pillow. He was breathing deeply, and there was a film of perspiration on his sun-darkened skin. The gray, fog-shrouded eyes were open, watching her intently as she turned her face to look at him.

"Trust you," he said very deliberately between long, recuperating breaths, "to blow all my plans to smithereens!"

Stacy, startled at the total unexpectedness of the wry comment, blinked. "What do you mean?"

"I should have known," he growled softly, "that any bride who would marry as part of a bargain and then show up for the wedding in a pair of jeans would find a way to ruin my wedding-night plans!"

Stacy licked her lower lip uncertainly. "What are you talking about, Hunter?" she whispered.

"I'm talking about how I was going to seduce and amaze you with my infinite finesse in the fine art of lovemaking. Show you that you could go crazy in my arms and I would know how to handle it. . . ."

Stacy frowned uncomprehendingly. "Hunter, this doesn't make any sense. I don't—"

"But what happens? At the last moment you start playing some very dangerous games. Teasing me, taunting me until I thought I'd go mad!" Hunter groaned, lifting himself up on one elbow and looking down into her face. "Does that settle the issue of my robotic self-control?" he demanded a little roughly, stroking her cheek with a finger. "Playing games with the devil is risky business, little flower witch. But I should have known that, too, is part of your nature."

He was right, Stacy realized with vague surprise as she studied the gray depths of his gaze. She did want to challenge him, lure him, make him aware only of her. He had succeeded in his goal tonight whether or not he fully realized it. She felt thoroughly bound to him in a way that admitted no rational explanation. It was far too primitive. But had she succeeded in accomplishing any part of her goal?

Stacy came awake early the next morning with a slow, languid stretch that was unexpectedly restricted by the weight of a man's arm across her middle. In an instant the memories of the night flooded into her consciousness as she turned to glance at her sleeping husband: memories of seemingly endless hours of passion and demand. It was as if, once unleashed, Hunter made no more attempt to control his desire and sensuous need. The devil might not yet know a human warmth in this most intimate of relationships, but Stacy knew she had unlocked one small door. Hunter Manning might have an unholy control over his temper, but he could not perfectly control his passion. He took from Stacy all she had to give and, in turn, withheld nothing of himself on that most primitive of levels.

Now, in the early desert light filtering in through the windows on the courtyard, Stacy gazed wonderingly into the sleep-softened face of her devil husband. The silver slash of hair tumbled amid the dark locks across his brow, giving him a thoroughly rakish look, even in sleep, and the hard, tough line of his body under the sheet was satisfying to her in the morning sunlight. Last night had unlocked more than one door, she admitted privately. Her own passion had been a revelation, even a little frightening. She had alternately teased and surrendered, fought and seduced, glorying in her newfound power. And Hunter had matched her at every turn, at times fiercely demanding, at others beguiling and seductive. Stacy realized that somehow they were a challenge to each other.

Hunter had made no secret of his satisfaction in mastering her after he had deliberately driven her wild, and he was always there at the heights with her, holding her close as they fell gently back to earth. Someday, Stacy told herself resolutely as she stirred and slipped out from under his arm, he would learn he wasn't in complete control.

"Don't tell me," Hunter suddenly said without opening his eyes, "you're an early riser."

Stacy winced. "I'm afraid so."

"I suppose it's only to be expected from a flower person," he remarked, his lashes lifting lazily to study her nude figure as she stood by the bed. The look deepened Stacy's already pink coloring, and she hurried to the closet that had been allotted to her on the day her belongings had arrived. Plunging inside, she brought out the Chinese-silk robe embroidered with huge, brilliant flowers against a dark background and flung it on.

"It's okay," he confided, watching her in some amusement. "I get up pretty early myself. There's not much else one can do out here on the desert when sunrise always

125

leaps out at you!" He sat up, the sheet falling back to reveal his smoothly muscled torso. Stacy fled with as much dignity as possible to the beautifully appointed bath.

"What would you like to do today?" Hunter asked with polite coolness half an hour later, digging into the ruby-red grapefruit Stacy had set in front of him. "You don't have to go to work, do you? We should give some semblance of enjoying our honeymoon!"

"No, I don't have to go in, although I usually do," she told him slowly. "A student from the University handles things on Saturday."

"Good," Hunter nodded, satisfied. "Then we'll spend the day together. Honeymoons are a time for getting to know one another, aren't they?" he added with a curiously challenging half-smile.

Stacy took a deep breath, determined to be as cool as her husband. "There is something I should probably take care of today. . . ."

"What's that?" He glanced up inquiringly.

"Well, I never got all my plants moved."

His eyes narrowed fractionally. "I just assumed you'd taken them to the nursery."

"I'm afraid not. I—I planned to move them here after I was sure—That is, after I found out whether or not—" She broke off helplessly, seeing the knowledge of what she was trying to say appear in Hunter's eyes.

"You weren't going to move your precious plants into your new home until you found out for certain it *was* going to be your home, is that it?" One dark brow lifted sardonically.

"Something like that."

"You could have asked me, Stacy," he chided a little grimly. "I would have told you there would be no question about it."

She shrugged, trying for an offhanded look. "Well, how was I to know you might not throw me out after you had finally talked to my father? If he'd called sometime before the wedding—"

"I would still have gone through with it," Hunter growled softly at her bent head.

"Even if you had realized before the marriage that I was—wasn't being totally forthright? . . ."

"Even," he stated bluntly, "if I had discovered that you were intent on tricking me. I'd already decided this bargain would suit me just fine, and I haven't changed my mind."

"I see," she whispered, not knowing what to make of his enigmatic statement. "Well, that leaves me with a lot of plants to move."

In the end they used Stacy's van to move the dozens of plants, retrieving it from where it had been left the day before in front of the nursery. Stacy checked in with the young man who managed the place on Saturdays and then drove with Hunter to the house she was vacating.

"I take it for every plant hanger stuck here in your ceiling, I'll have to install one in mine—ours," he corrected at once as he carefully lifted down the huge fern in the hall of the little house.

Stacy, her arms full of pots, paused to peer up at him where he stood on a small stool. "Will you mind?" she asked a little anxiously. Not everyone, she had learned, liked being surrounded by greenery to the extent she did.

He grinned at her, the fern in one strong fist. "I'll put them in on one condition." The sudden humor surprised her.

"What's that?" she demanded suspiciously.

"That you don't go changing your mind after we've located a plant. I'm not about to have that house studded with lots of little hooks from which nothing is hanging because you didn't like the way the plant looked in that particular corner!"

"Don't worry," she told him bracingly. "Your house is going to love my plants!"

Sometime later Stacy handed up the last of the hanging plants for Hunter, once again on a small stool, to position in front of a section of courtyard windows. She stepped back to eye the effect and nodded with satisfaction.

"That looks perfect! It will get all the light it needs, but the courtyard will provide enough shade to keep it from getting burned."

"Somehow," Hunter observed, jumping lightly from the stool and glancing around at his handiwork, "I never envisioned spending my honeymoon turning my home into a greenhouse!"

Stacy slanted him a long green glance. "I think my plants do a lot for this place. And the, uh, greenhouse comes on Monday. . . ."

"What are you talking about? That huge thing in your old backyard?" he demanded, his dark head swiveling around to confront her. "That doesn't go with the rental?"

"I'm afraid not," she admitted humbly. "But you don't have to worry about moving it. I'll borrow some help and some tools from the nursery on Monday afternoon. It will be in before you know it!" Seeing his look of rueful resignation, she added quickly, "You know, I must say I would never have suspected you of being so good with your hands. I mean, you don't look like the type who cares much about little home projects such as putting in plant hooks." Her appreciative glance went to the small hammer he still held in one hand.

"What type do I look like, Stacy?" he said with a sudden, quirking smile as he set down the hammer and dusted

128

off his hands on his jeans. His foggy eyes met hers with curious intentness and Stacy swallowed in nervous reaction for no good reason.

"Well," she hesitated and then said slowly, "the first time I saw you on my brother's patio, I thought to myself that you could have been cast in a Western film."

"Playing the good guy in the white hat, I trust," he said, chuckling.

"Not quite." She grinned back, seeing the humor in his eyes. "I envisioned you more as the marauding gunslinger riding into town and bringing trouble with him. A black hat, definitely!"

He stepped forward, raising a hand to cup her chin, and the gray eyes gleamed down into hers. "I didn't do much to make you change your first impression, did I? A gunslinging devil. Is that really how you see me?"

There was a question in his eyes, a question Stacy knew needed to be answered. She parted her lips, unable to look away from the demand, and was on the point of saying something, exactly what she wasn't certain, when the phone rang.

The fragile moment was shattered at once, and Hunter dropped his fingers.

"I'll get it," Stacy offered, hurrying toward the phone with a strange sense of relief. "Your hands are filthy!"

She was aware of his negligent shrug as he walked toward the kitchen sink to rinse his dirt-stained hands.

"Hello?" Stacy said quickly, wondering if she was going to have to introduce herself as Hunter's wife to the caller. Most people probably didn't know he was married yet.

. . .

"Stacy? This is Leana. Happy honeymoon!" There was a curious, almost forced quality in her sister-in-law's voice that brought a small frown to Stacy's forehead.

"Hi, Leana. I wasn't expecting to hear from you. . . ."

"I know, darling. But I really did want to do something for you and Hunter. He absolutely refused to let Eric and me do anything except stand up with you at the wedding, and then he whisked you away so quickly. . . ." There was a question in her voice that Stacy chose to ignore. "At any rate," Leana went on immediately, "I want to have the two of you over for dinner this week. Is Hunter there? I expect he'll be the one I'll have to convince. Let me talk to him, darling."

Stacy hesitated, not liking the barely restrained eagerness in Leana's request. But she couldn't very well say Hunter wasn't there, could she?

Putting a hand over the mouthpiece, Stacy turned toward the kitchen and saw her husband lounging in the doorway, watching her as he dried his hands on a towel. His brow kicked upward in mute question as he caught her look.

"It's—it's Leana," Stacy whispered quietly. "She wants to talk to you. Something about having us over for dinner." She held out the phone, not knowing what else to do.

"Tell her I'm busy. If you really want to accept the invitation, go ahead," he told her laconically and turned back to the kitchen.

Stacy blinked, surprised. "Leana?" she spoke quickly. "Hunter's too busy to come to the phone right now, but he says we'll be able to make it for dinner. . . ." Lord knew that was the last thing Stacy wanted in that moment, but she couldn't think of any genuine excuse for turning down the offer. And she didn't want to hurt her brother's feelings.

"I see." There was a definite measure of disappointment

in Leana's voice. "Well, in that case, why don't we make it for Monday night. Will that be all right with you?"

"Yes, that will be fine. Do you—do you want me to bring the main course or something?"

"What? Oh, you mean because of your weird diet? No, don't worry about that. I'll just turn the whole thing over to Maria. She'll think of something. She always does. We'll probably have Mexican food, of course. I think she mentioned once that there are a lot of meatless Mexican dishes," Leana noted vaguely, sounding anxious to get off the phone now. "See you Monday night around six."

Stacy slowly replaced the phone and walked toward the kitchen, where she found Hunter peering interestedly into the refrigerator.

"Anything fit for lunch among all these roots and berries?" he demanded, sensing her quiet presence behind him.

"I think I can put something together. I don't exactly starve to death on a daily basis," Stacy observed, coming forward to edge him aside and take command at the refrigerator.

"You know," Hunter noted almost absently, watching as she put together some huge cheese and sprout sandwiches, "that brother of yours had better make a serious move to bring his wife to heel, or he's going to be in real trouble."

Stacy looked up from her work, startled. She had been thinking about Leana's eagerness to talk to Hunter and wondering if the younger woman was still harboring fantasies. "I'm sure she was just . . . just being friendly," she said flatly, feeling some vague need to defend her sister-in-law.

"She's a born flirt," Hunter corrected bluntly. "And

Eric had better do something about it before it gets out of hand."

"I'm—I'm sure you're exaggerating. . . ."

"Like hell I am." There was a sardonic twist to the words.

Stacy felt her temper flicker alive. "You would know, I suppose. After all, it wasn't too long ago that you could have cared less about my brother's marriage!"

"Things have changed," he retorted coolly and then grinned abruptly at the gathering frown on her face. "Don't look at me like that when you're holding a knife in one hand!"

"Hunter," Stacy said carefully, "sometimes you make me very annoyed."

"I've noticed," he drawled, reaching out to pick up the plate of sandwiches and carry them over to the breakfast nook. "But I gather from what your father said on the phone last night that I'm not unique!"

"My father is referring to my past," Stacy declared firmly, following him with a tray of sliced fruit.

"Your recent past, I expect?"

"No! I've been doing very well handling my temper these past few years," she told him forcefully.

"Until you met me?" he prodded interestedly as they sat down.

"Stop laughing at me!"

"It's okay, honey, your temper doesn't frighten me," he assured her, helping himself to a fat sandwich. "I've got one of my own."

Stacy stared at him, chewing on her lip thoughtfully. "Do you . . ." she began delicately, wondering how to ask, "I mean, have you ever lost it? Really lost it? I know you've threatened to a couple of times, but somehow, in the end, you always seem to be able to control it.

132

. . ." She broke off a little wistfully, wishing she had the same ability. She thought she'd learned to master herself, but there had been times lately . . .

"What's the matter?" He grinned around a mouthful of sandwich. "Afraid I'll go crazy with rage and beat you?"

She met his eyes across the short distance between them and considered that. "No," she announced finally with great certainty, although she could not have said why she was so sure of her answer. "I'm not afraid you'll go into a wild rage and really hurt me." Then she chuckled ruefully. "But I can see you threatening to beat me again like you did that first night."

"Oh, I can see myself doing more than just threatening," he assured her with a gleaming look. "Given the right set of circumstances, I expect I could quite cheerfully make certain you'd be unable to sit down for a week!"

"But you wouldn't do it while foaming at the mouth with anger, is that it?" She smiled, beginning to enjoy the banter.

"Not at all. I'd do it with considered deliberation and out of a sense of responsibility toward the stability of our marriage! The same way," Hunter abruptly added, "that your brother should beat his wife!"

"Hunter!" Stacy's humor was wiped out in an instant. "Is that your solution to my brother and Leana's problems?"

"Yes," he stated emphatically and then waved a hand dismissingly. "But I don't feel like talking about them right now. What would you like to do after lunch?"

Stacy frowned, on the one hand wanting to argue him out of his conviction about how Eric ought to solve his marital problems, and on the other wanting to do something besides wrangle with her new husband on this the first full day of their marriage. The desire to spend a peaceful afternoon with him won out. She was sure there would be battles enough in the future.

"Have you seen much of Tucson since you moved back?" she asked hesitantly. "I know you've been here almost two months, but you've probably been quite busy. What with all your scheming and everything," she couldn't resist adding.

His eyes narrowed for a split second, and she thought he would make a somewhat nasty retort. But he didn't. Instead he smiled. "Thinking of giving me a tour of the town?"

"Well, perhaps a few of the fun things. That is, if you'd like to. . . ."

"Sounds great."

With a peculiar sense of unreality Stacy watched the warm afternoon slip by as she took him first to the Arizona-Sonora Desert Museum, a unique living museum where a tremendous variety of desert animals were featured in a natural habitat. Mountain lions, snakes, bighorn sheep, prairie dogs, and a fascinating collection of desert cats prowled and ate and worked in front of entranced visitors.

"It seems more like a zoo to me than a museum." Stacy smiled, leaning over a fence to watch some otters frolicking in a canyon-type stream. "I always think of museums as places for nonliving things."

"And you're very much into living creatures, aren't you?" Hunter noted, his eyes on her enthusiastic face as she watched the animals below. "I'm probably lucky you're not bringing a collection of cats and dogs and hamsters into the house along with all those plants!"

Stacy laughed. "At one time I was torn between critters and plants. My room was a combination zoo and conservatory when I was growing up. But finally the plants won out, at least as far as making career plans went. . . ." Her voice trailed off as she remembered the endless scenes that decision had entailed.

"Parents didn't approve?" Hunter asked softly, standing with his arm draped in careless possession around her waist, one foot resting on the bottom rail of a fence.

Stacy shook her head ruefully. "They had . . . other plans for me."

"Such as?" he pressed.

"Such as a proper school where I would learn the social graces Mom had despaired of being able to teach me herself, and then a proper marriage with the son of one of my father's friends." Stacy sighed softly. "I'm afraid I was a constant disappointment to my family," she admitted wryly.

"If it's any consolation, I didn't do much better," he remarked quietly.

Stacy looked up in surprise. "I thought you said your father was grooming you to take over his business until my father bought him out."

"He was. But I had other plans. I'd *always* had other plans," he muttered. "And I didn't care much for having my life preordained, I'm afraid."

"Did you . . . did you fight a lot with your father?" Stacy couldn't resist asking gently, turning to watch his hard profile.

"Constantly. I left home to make my own way when I was barely seventeen."

"I moved out when I was eighteen. I think by then Mom and Dad had pretty much given up on me. When I refused to even consider dating the man they had selected, they just threw up their hands and said the hell with it. They'd done their best."

"But we both were there when the chips were down,"

135

Hunter mused grimly. "When I found out what was happening to my father's business, I forgot all about my pride and came pleading to your father. And when you thought I would hurt your family, you made deals with the devil! The funny part is, I don't think either of our fathers would have appreciated our efforts!" he concluded ruefully. "In his own way, my parent was at least as arrogant as yours."

They stood together in a close silence, not speaking and not feeling the need to do so. A delicate, sensitive communion hovered in the air for a moment, and then Stacy shook herself free of it and turned away.

"On to Old Tucson," she ordered with brisk, determined cheerfulness. "I want to show you how you would have looked and where you would have lived if you'd been born in the proper century!"

"A hundred years ago?" he chuckled.

"At least!"

CHAPTER SEVEN

The tour of Old Tucson, a recreation of the rip-roaring town as it was in the middle of the eighteen hundreds, used up most of what was left of the afternoon. Stacy privately decided her husband looked quite at home against the rough Western backdrop.

"They use this place for filming Westerns," Stacy explained as a stagecoach loaded with delighted youngsters rolled past. Then she halted her explanation as she spied activity up ahead. "Hurry," she ordered, grabbing his hand. "We don't want to miss the big gunfight!"

"Sadistic little thing, aren't you?" Hunter observed, increasing his stride but refusing to run as she wanted him to do.

"I'm just displaying an interest in our heritage," Stacy told him haughtily.

He laughed and allowed himself to be pulled along the movie-set street to where two grim-faced men in Western garb were facing off in the classic, violent fashion. Stacy almost forgot herself and booed when the good guy won.

The unexpected magic of the day seemed to linger on through dinner, a spicy vegetable curry, which Hunter attacked at first with wariness and then enthusiasm. Later he produced a clear, potent liqueur with a small flourish, put a set of Vivaldi concertos on the intimidatingly sophisticated stereo, and pulled Stacy lightly down beside him on the leather couch.

"I'm in a mood to seduce a witch tonight," he warned in a deep, delicious voice that sent pleasant shivers along her nerve endings. He pulled her close against his side and put the small liqueur glass in her fingers. As their hands made contact, Stacy's eyes collided and were caught in the treacherous mists of his gaze, and she found herself suddenly and horribly shy.

"Do you like Vivaldi?" he murmured as she curled her denim-covered legs under her. His fingers toyed with the familiar loose knot of her hair.

"Oh, yes," she assured him. "But I don't have anything that elaborate to play my records on, I'm afraid." She indicated the beautiful stereo in the corner with all its space-age sleekness and gadgetry. "I've left my machine packed. There's no sense pulling it out and embarrassing it by putting it next to yours!"

"I like good, sophisticated machines." He half-smiled, sipping from his glass as he watched her face.

"I've noticed," she said wryly. "All the appliances in the house, your stereo equipment, your car. They're all first-class. It must be the design instinct in you." Stacy knew she was becoming chatty and didn't fully understand why. Good heavens! She had already shared this man's bed once, why was she nervous?

"And I have married a first-class witch," he whispered, removing the glass from her hand and bending close as he set it down on the table.

Stacy swallowed, aware of the foretaste of the passion he would soon be stirring in her. Her lashes fluttered shut as his mouth descended to hers, and she gave a tiny, almost inaudible moan as he used his weight to push her gently against the back of the couch. Her hands went up to settle lightly on his shoulders.

"Are you pleased with your bargain, Stacy Manning?" he ground out against her lips an instant before forcing them apart with the insistent tip of his tongue. She had no chance to answer then as she found herself engaged in a small, intimate duel that fanned the already glowing embers of her desire. Perhaps it was just as well she couldn't respond verbally, a voice in her head observed, because under the impetus of her growing need she might have whispered the truth: that she wasn't fully satisfied and wouldn't be until he learned he couldn't use people the way he used machines.

Her fingers twisted in his hair, thrusting through the darkness of it with intense pleasure and feeling him reciprocate by putting one hand to the insecurely pinned redbrown stuff of her curls and yanking them gently free. As it tumbled down to Stacy's shoulders Hunter buried his face in it for a long moment.

"You remind me of your own nursery," he growled heavily. "Fresh and green and natural. My own private garden. Will you tease me and mock me again tonight when I try to open the gate?"

"Perhaps," she whispered daringly, shivering with delight as he kissed the exquisitely vulnerable area behind her ear. "Will you mind if I do?"

"Not in the least," he assured her with masterful male disregard for the little games a woman might choose to play. "It will all come to the same thing in the end."

She breathed a small, half-rueful sigh. "Is it me or yourself you're so sure of, Hunter?"

"Will you lose that temper of yours if I tell you the truth?" he teased, his fingers at work on the buttons of her begonia-splashed shirt.

"Possibly. But I thought you weren't afraid of my temper," she retorted, her short-nailed fingers kneading the muscles of his shoulders.

He chuckled wickedly, finding the softness of her breasts with his questing hand. "I'm not afraid of it, but at the moment there are other things I'd rather do than tame it. A man should never turn down a challenge from his woman though, so I'll tell you the truth." His thumb was on the delicate tip of her breast now, enticing the nipple into a growing awareness. Stacy shifted restlessly beneath his weight. "The answer," he told her softly, "is that I'm sure of both of us. Your sweet surrender last night told me all I needed to know about you, and I know what you do to me. I also know I couldn't abide having you do that for another man," he added in a rough, gravelly voice. "A man can very quickly become somewhat possessive, it seems!"

"Possessive?" she queried, unfastening the buttons of his shirt and sliding her palms inside, relishing the feel of his chest and the hardness of his body. She didn't want to be possessed, she told herself, she wanted to be loved! "That sounds a little primitive."

"It is," he whispered thickly and uttered a tight, impatient male groan of desire as he felt her fingers exploring the contours of his body down to the waistband of his jeans. "You seem to have a knack," he said, gritting his teeth, "for bringing out the primitive in me!"

Stacy, enjoying her small moment of power, smiled up at him through her lashes when he lifted his head to gaze heatedly down at her. "Nonsense," she teased. "A man like you is always in control of himself!"

He gave a crack of almost savage laughter at that, uncoiling rapidly to his feet and reaching down to scoop her up from the couch. "You tease the devil at your own peril, witch," he warned, carrying her down the hall with swift, strong strides. "I'll show you what happens to little flower witches who think they can hide behind locked gates and play games!"

Stacy looked up at him with glittering green eyes, responding to the overwhelming masculinity of him and wanting to goad and provoke and entice him until he could do nothing but respond to her. He brought out something primitive in her, just as he claimed she did to him. When she met the shifting, stormy gray fog of his gaze and found herself once again lost in that chartless world, nothing seemed to matter but clinging safely to the rocklike strength he represented, clinging until neither of them could escape.

"Hunter, darling Hunter," she breathed as he tossed her lightly down on the bed and followed heavily, his body pinning hers to the sheets. "Do you always take what you want?"

"I've wanted few things as badly as I've wanted this!" he told her in a deep, positive tone, and then his mouth was on hers again, drugging her into a state where all that mattered to her senses was the warm, hard feel of the man who seemed to cover every inch of her body with his own.

It was only much later when Stacy lay quietly in his arms, drifting toward sleep, that she remembered his words and wondered whether it was herself or the revenge she represented that Hunter claimed to want so badly.

Monday afternoon Stacy grimly and determinedly attacked the last, remaining task that would make the move into Hunter's home complete. Disassembling and reassembling the orchid greenhouse was not something she looked forward to at all. She knew it was going to be horribly complicated, and when she finally found the instructions that had originally come with the greenhouse kit she almost threw them away in exasperation. Who could follow all those little lines and diagrams?

Still, with the willing assistance of two young men who worked part-time at the nursery, the greenhouse finally collapsed and was loaded into the van. The nearly two hundred beautiful orchid plants that had been inside had been carefully transported earlier.

"I have the impression," John, the student from the University who normally helped out on Saturday, remarked, "that getting this thing together again is going to be more difficult than taking it apart. You should have hired a mathematics major or somebody studying architecture," he added morosely as the three of them stood amid the piles of rubble that supposedly constituted a greenhouse. "Not a couple of liberal arts types!" He ran a hand through his shaggy sandy-brown hair and looked ruefully at his fellow student.

"I suppose the best approach," Neal, his long brown hair held out of his eyes with a tennis-style sweatband, observed, "is for us to handle the manual labor while Stacy reads off the instructions."

"I was afraid you were going to say that," Stacy groaned, poring over the crumpled diagrams with a fierce frown. "Well, we'd better decide exactly where it's going to go, first. I get the feeling that you're not going to want to shift it a few feet if I'm not thrilled with the way it looks after it's up!"

An hour later a deeply amused male voice interrupted Stacy's disgusted concentration on her diagrams, and she looked up from her cross-legged sitting position to find Hunter rounding the corner of the house into the backyard, his suit jacket slung over one arm and a leather briefcase in his other hand.

"What the hell is going on here?" he demanded, surveying the shambles of a greenhouse, the two sweating, straining young men heaving on a post, and his rumpled, stained wife sitting in the middle of a heap of plastic and wood components she had, as yet, been unable to identify. "Are you reconstructing the last World's Fair?"

"Oh, Hunter!" Stacy wailed, leaping dejectedly to her feet. "It's all a horrible mess! I was so hoping to have it put together by the time you got home from work! Now I don't think it's ever going to work. I'll probably have to buy a new one!" She threw the battered papers in her hands onto the ground with a disgusted gesture and then planted her fists on her hips.

Neal and John, gratefully aware of the presence of another man, even if he were dressed in a suit, dropped the post with which they had been struggling and came forward hopefully.

"Just out of curiosity," Hunter remarked with a suspicious quirk of his lips that told Stacy he was on the verge of laughing outright. "How did you get it together the first time?" He walked toward her, peering interestedly at the various bits and pieces lying on the ground.

"The company I bought it from erected it." She sighed sadly. "But they promised me it would be easy to handle on my own when I was ready to move!"

"I guess we should have labeled the various parts when we tore it down, huh, Mr. Manning?" John suggested, shaking his head.

Stacy suddenly remembered her manners. "Hunter, this is Neal Rhodes and John Finley. They both work for me part-time. They were kind enough to give me a hand this afternoon."

"I told her she should have hired some nonliberal-arts

143

majors." John grinned as Hunter set down his briefcase to shake hands. "What do you think? Any hope?"

Stacy frowned for a moment as she realized Neal and John were instinctively turning to the older man for advice. What made them think Hunter would know anything about putting together a greenhouse? But she knew the answer to that even as Hunter handed her his jacket and bent down to retrieve the pages of assembly diagrams. There was an air of competency and authority about her husband that younger men such as her assistants reacted to automatically.

There was an atmosphere of expectancy among the three would-be greenhouse builders as they watched Hunter glance through the diagrams and then walk briefly around the piles of parts. Stacy could almost feel Neal's and John's inner sighs of relief when her husband nodded his dark head once and glanced up.

"Okay, Neal, you take that sheet of plastic there, and John, grab that post over there. Not that one, the other one," Hunter instructed. The students bent to their assigned tasks with a new attitude of eagerness, and Stacy stood by hopefully, Hunter's coat over her arm, his briefcase at her feet.

"Stacy, honey, why don't you go inside and bring out three beers?" he suggested kindly, pausing to drop an absently possessive little kiss on her upturned nose.

Stacy saw John and Neal grin happily at the request, and she frowned hesitantly at her husband.

"I'm not sure they're of age yet," she whispered worriedly. "Perhaps juice?"

"Neal and John," Hunter told her succinctly, "are both doing men's work, and they are entitled to some of the few privileges left to the male of the species. Go get the beers!"

Stacy caught the appreciative glances of her workers,

knew her husband was completely established as a hero, and grinned in rueful defeat. She couldn't fight that; didn't want to. She fled toward the house to fetch the beers.

A long time later, enroute to Eric and Leana's home for dinner, Stacy sent a smiling glance across the car to Hunter. "You know," she said, chuckling, "you're really going to be quite useful around the place! I can't tell you how grateful I am for the rescue of my greenhouse!"

Hunter threw her a sardonic grin, shifting gears in the powerful sports car with smooth expertise. "I have the feeling you would have been equally grateful to anyone who happened along in time to salvage things. But that's all right, I won't fight my luck. I'll collect full payment from my adoring wife tonight when we get home!"

"Have you always been able to do that sort of thing?" she pressed curiously, ignoring his teasing. "Working with diagrams and hardware and knowing how things are supposed to go together?" She thought again of the efficient way he had hung her plants without marring the woodwork or ceiling and the fact that he had designed his home from scratch. He surrounded himself with quality machines where machines were needed and knew how to take care of them. All matters that were foreign to her nature.

He shrugged. "I've always been interested in the way things work, and I've had enough practical experience over the years to be able to pick up something as simple as that greenhouse diagram and figure out what the designers intended."

"Simple! Those little squares and lines were driving me crazy!" Stacy confessed with a laugh.

"On the other hand," Hunter said softly, slanting her a warm glance, "I doubt that I could get even a weed to grow. Your abilities and skills are different than mine, Stacy, and just as amazing to me."

145

Stacy felt herself become suffused with a pleasant glow at the outright compliment, a glow that vanished the moment her brother, Eric, opened the door. Instantly she knew something was wrong.

"Good evening, Hunter," Eric said politely, his face wearing the right expression for a genial host as he shook hands with his new brother-in-law. "Good to see you two. Come on inside. Leana's waiting with drinks." He bent down and gave Stacy a quick, affectionate hug. "You've done all right for yourself, Sister," he murmured in her ear. "I must admit I had a few doubts last week when you announced you were getting married, but not anymore. You look very happy."

Stacy, unaware she appeared any different than usual, blushed.

"What about you, Eric?" she whispered as Hunter stepped past them to greet Leana and take the drink she was holding out. "Is everything all right with you?" She saw that Leana had made herself up with more than the usual care this evening, and she saw, too, the added warmth in the other woman's eyes when she greeted Hunter.

"I'm fine, Stacy, just fine," Eric said quickly, putting a drink into his sister's hand, and Stacy knew at once he was lying.

"Stacy, darling, I'm honored," Leana mocked lightly. "You put on a dress for my little party!"

"You should be pleased." Stacy smiled dutifully, not liking the strange brittleness in her sister-in-law's words. "It's one of the only three dresses I own!"

Hunter glanced at his wife's simple, fitted black dress patterned in huge yellow and orange orchids and chuckled. "And all three have flowers on them, just like all her shirts!"

But none of the three dresses, Stacy thought grimly, were cut as daringly and as provocatively as the sapphire-blue hostess gown Leana wore tonight. It struck her admittedly unsophisticated senses as being too much for an evening at home with relatives. And one of Leana's skills was in knowing exactly what to wear for any occasion.

"What with all the rush of the wedding," Leana began brightly as she passed around a plate of hors d'oeuvres, "and you must admit it was a bit hurried," she added chidingly, "I didn't get a chance to find out if you two have plans to take time off from work for a honeymoon."

Stacy, concentrating intently on dipping a carrot stick in the cheese spread, said nothing. Let Hunter answer that one!

"Oh, we'll get around to it," her husband replied dismissingly. "I thought I'd take Stacy down to Acapulco in a couple of months."

Stacy did glance up at that. It was certainly the first she'd heard of any such plan!

"That sounds marvelous," Leana said enthusiastically, glancing significantly at Eric. "Eric and I haven't been out of Tucson since he took over Rylan Enterprises. It would be great to get away. . . ." She let the sentence trail off on a wistful note that was apparent to everyone. Eric smiled a rueful smile, and Stacy saw his glance go to Hunter, as if appealing for some masculine understanding. To her complete astonishment, he got it.

"It's going to take some time to settle down into a position like the one you've got, Eric," Hunter said easily. "If you don't put in the time that needs to go into the business in the beginning, you'll never be able to make up for it later, as I'm sure you realize."

Something in Eric's face lightened just a fraction as he nodded in agreement and then took a sip of his drink.

"Right now it feels like a twenty-four-hour-a-day job! And the problems never stop coming. For some strange reason the technical side of things is turning out to be the easiest part to manage. It's the people side of the business that's getting to me. I guess, although I'd never thought much about it, I'm basically a little different in my approach than Dad was," he added almost hesitantly, his eyes going to his sister's.

"Stacy tells me the job is yours now. Completely," Hunter said softly, meaningfully. "You have no need to do things exactly the way your father did."

"I suppose not," Eric said slowly with a small frown. "But it's hard to argue with success, and Dad was nothing if not successful!"

"I take it," Hunter said perceptively, "you're in a position where your instincts tell you to go one way, and you can almost hear your father looking over your shoulder and telling you to handle it a different way."

Eric grinned. "You've hit it right on the nose."

"Are you two going to talk business all evening?" Leana demanded with a small, charming pout.

"Uh, Leana, why don't we go check on Maria and see how things are going in the kitchen?" Stacy suggested hastily, getting to her feet. "Perhaps we could help out by setting the table or something, and I've been wanting to ask how your party went last weekend. I hope I didn't cause too big a scene appearing out of nowhere in my jeans. . . ." Before the younger woman could respond, Stacy had her firmly by the arm and was leading her off toward the kitchen. Eric needed someone to talk to just then, and Hunter seemed willing to act as a sounding board. She wasn't certain why he should be so generous, but she wasn't going to ruin the opportunity, either. She hadn't liked the tension in her brother's face this evening, and it was obvious Leana was not overly sympathetic.

"Honestly," Leana complained as she allowed herself to be led out of the living room, although not without a last, pleading glance over her shoulder to Hunter, who ignored it. "That brother of yours! It seems all he can talk about lately is business! Things were different before he took over control. I wish . . ." her voice trailed off wistfully.

"Have you tried letting him talk to you about it?" Stacy inquired quietly as they stepped through the dining room into the elegant kitchen. "Perhaps if you—"

"Oh, Stacy, Rylan Enterprises is the last thing I want to hear about when he gets home from work! Besides—"

"Ah! *La Señora* Manning!" A large person waving a ladle and wearing a white apron whisked toward Stacy, enveloping her in a huge hug. "Señora Rylan told me of the wedding! I am so happy for you! I have seen your man. . . ." Maria paused, grinning down into Stacy's face and gesturing significantly with the ladle. Without a pause she slipped into Spanish. "He is very much a man, no? I thought the first time I met him there was some of the devil in him, but there is that in such men. And I think you will make him happy. You are now *La Señora de las Flores!* No longer *La Señorita de las Flores!*"

Flower lady. Stacy chuckled in spite of herself, thinking of how Hunter had called her that more than once. "Thank you, Maria. I appreciate your good wishes," she said in English. "Leana and I have come to help. Shall we set the table?"

"*Sí, sí! Muchas gracias, señora.*" Maria waved them cheerfully on about the task, smiling happily as she saw Stacy sniff delightedly at the makings for cheese enchiladas, tostadas, and a variety of other good things. "No meat!" she assured Stacy, beaming. "I remember from the time you ate here once before on Señor Rylan's birthday!"

"Thanks, Maria." Stacy laughed.

"I suppose we'd better get going if we're ever to get the table set," Leana told her sister-in-law petulantly, handing her a stack of napkins. Without a word Stacy followed her out into the dining room, where the two women worked in silence for a long moment. And then Leana said coolly, with a sidelong glance, "When's the baby due?"

Stacy blinked in astonishment, staring at the younger woman. "What?" she managed, completely taken aback.

"Oh, come on, Stacy, there's no need to pretend. It's obvious!"

"It is?" Stacy glanced down at her flat stomach and smiled wryly. "Leana, I hate to disappoint you, but I'm not pregnant!" Her gaze lifted to meet her sister-in-law's narrowed blue eyes.

"Why else," Leana inquired with great casualness, "would Hunter have married you?"

Stacy felt the red flood into her face, and a wave of anger swept along her nerve endings. She wondered what Leana would say if she told her the truth. That Stacy had bargained with Hunter to keep him from destroying the younger woman's marriage. Perhaps Leana wouldn't be the least bit grateful! But it was really Eric Stacy had wanted to protect. Eric, who loved his lovely, selfish wife.

"I assure you, it wasn't for that reason," Stacy said flatly, resuming her chore.

"I know he never had any intention of marriage, right up until the night of the party, when you made your grand announcement," Leana whispered grimly. "He had probably been seeing you casually, but until you ran into him on the patio and told him you were pregnant, I assure you he wasn't planning to marry you. Is that the real reason

150

you came back to the house that night, Stacy? Because you knew Hunter would be there and you wanted to trap him with the news?"

Stacy's rising anger put her suddenly on the offensive. "How do you know Hunter wasn't planning on marriage, Leana?" There! Let her sister-in-law wriggle out of that one!

"Hunter and I had grown rather close," Leana said with great dignity. "We . . . we understand each other, you see."

"Perhaps if you made more of an effort to understand Eric . . ." Stacy let her words trail off meaningfully, taking a certain satisfaction in the spots of color that appeared in Leana's cheeks.

She never learned what the other woman might have said next, however, because Maria threw open the kitchen door and informed them that dinner was ready and told them to fetch the men, as men never liked waiting for their food.

It was Stacy who walked back into the living room to make the announcement, and she paused a moment before Hunter and Eric glanced up from their conversation. Eric's expression had changed, she decided with some relief. There was a thoughtfulness in his eyes now, rather than the look of tension that had been there earlier.

"I agree," he was saying quietly to Hunter. "I know Dad would say fire the man and the hell with it. But you can't do that to someone who's devoted most of his working life to your firm."

"Your idea of shifting the responsibilities is a good one." Hunter nodded encouragingly. "Correctly handled, Winthrop will see himself as adviser to up-and-coming junior management. And I'm sure he still has a lot to contribute in that capacity, judging from what you've told me. But he needs to get away from the stress of directly managing production work."

"Yes, I think you're right. I appreciate the chance to talk it over with you. One of the things I'm learning is that it can be a bit lonely in my position. I have to be careful about taking people who work for me into my confidence when it comes to dealing with their co-workers. That sort of thing would cause havoc and jealousy in no time!" He looked up then, saw Stacy, and smiled.

"I must say, Sister dear, I'm awfully glad you decided to marry Hunter, here, rather than that philosophy-spouting bookshop owner you introduced me to that day I dropped by the nursery to pick up flowers for Leana. It's going to be great having someone else in the family to talk big business with besides Dad. Not that I don't like discussing things with my father," he added quickly to Hunter. "But he does have a rather rigid point of view on most subjects. One doesn't really discuss things with him so much as receive advice, I'm learning as I grow older. I think it's a lesson Stacy learned before she was out of the cradle!"

Stacy, who had seen her husband's eyes narrow slightly at mention of Gary Bowen, interrupted quickly to tell them dinner was ready.

A long time later during the drive home, Stacy forced herself to consider the evening from a strictly logical viewpoint. There was no doubt that Hunter had made an admiring friend in her brother. And her husband had totally ignored Leana's small glances and meaningful innuendos at the dinner table. She could understand his being willing to ignore her sister-in-law; after all, he'd given his word not to disrupt the marriage when Stacy had made the bargain. But why would he go out of his way to be especially friendly and helpful to Eric?

152

"What's on your mind, Stacy?" Hunter asked softly as he guided the car through evening traffic. "You're awfully quiet over there."

"I—I was just thinking about the evening," she admitted.

"Worried about Leana's behavior?" He smiled grimly. "Eric sure as hell ought to be concerned about it!"

"She, uh, seems to think you and she had—had something of an understanding before you married me," Stacy replied evenly.

"Oh, I understand her, all right," he growled. "It's just too bad your brother doesn't! Out with it, though. What particularly did she say to upset you this evening? You had a strange look in your eyes when you came through the door to announce dinner."

"It was nothing, really. . . ."

"Stacy!"

She shrugged. Why not tell him? His reaction might be interesting. "Leana had just finished suggesting that the reason for our marriage was that I was—was—" The sentence had started off well, but somehow it was proving difficult to end!

"That you were what?" Hunter demanded gently.

"Pregnant," Stacy concluded bluntly, her eyes on the night view out the car window. There was a suspiciously long pause from the other side of the vehicle.

"Perhaps," Hunter finally said in a low, neutral tone, "you are. Now."

"No!" Stacy's head swung around in shock, and her green eyes glittered as she glared at his profile.

He tossed her a strange, quirking smile. "You don't like children?"

"I have nothing against children," she snapped, abruptly infuriated. How could he be so casual about something like this? "But I certainly wouldn't want them born into a situation where the only thing holding the parents together is the father's need for revenge!"

"I see," he stated, still in that strange neutral voice. "But perhaps it will happen anyway. You know I'm not taking any precautions, flower lady," he added gently. "And I hadn't noticed you—"

"A woman," Stacy declared tightly, seethingly, "can take care of herself."

With a suddenness that was startling, Hunter swerved out of traffic, coming to a neat, efficient, totally unexpected halt alongside the curb.

"Hunter! What are you doing?" Stacy gasped as he switched off the engine and turned to confront her, his arm flung along the back of the seat. In the confines of the sleek vehicle's cockpit he seemed larger and more menacing than usual. The lights of the well-instrumented dash reflected starkly from the shaft of silver in his dark hair, and the gray eyes were dark, threatening pools.

"If you're planning on handling any unwanted complications of this marriage by having an abortion, you can damn well forget it!" he grated, not touching her.

Stacy stared at him, wide-eyed, and suddenly it all made sense. "You wouldn't mind in the least if I got pregnant, would you?" she whispered in heavy comprehension, her heart sinking.

"The thought of you having my baby doesn't bother me in the slightest," he confirmed, giving emphasis to each word.

Stacy swallowed, battling fiercely to hold back tears of despair and rage. He had said his revenge would be a subtle one. It wasn't until now that she had fully understood. "You needn't worry about my having an abortion," she bit out evenly. "I went to a doctor last week and got some pills." At least he would know she didn't intend to cooperate completely in his plan of revenge!

"Why didn't you tell me?" he snapped.

"I didn't see that it was any of your business!"

"My God, woman! You try a man's patience! How dare you leave me out of a decision as basic as this?"

"If you were really concerned about the matter, you would have brought it up yourself. Before the marriage!" she hissed angrily.

She saw him take a visible grip on himself, and once again he demonstrated his annoying ability to handle his own temper. It was clear she had upset his plans, and he was furious, but he wasn't going to pursue the battle tonight. She wondered why.

"I don't like the idea of you being on the pill," Hunter stated categorically.

Stacy smiled grimly to herself but said nothing.

"We are both, however, too upset to discuss the subject reasonably tonight. So we'll wait and do it another time." Hunter switched on the engine with a vicious little gesture that gave evidence of his emotional state. "And don't think," he added gratingly as he glanced into the side mirror before pulling back out into traffic, "that I'm going to let this matter ride. We'll settle it soon!"

With a deep breath of regret and sadness, Stacy sank heavily back into the leather seat, her fingers clenched tightly in her lap. She had won this small round, but she had paid a terrible price. For now she fully comprehended the nature of her husband's revenge. It all made sense: the way he had made a deliberate effort to cement Eric's friendship tonight; his desire for her to have a child.

Paul J. Rylan might shrug and write off the loss of his wayward, difficult daughter, but he wouldn't be nearly so dispassionate about the defection of his son and heir.

When he discovered that Eric looked on the enemy as a friend and business confidant, the senior Rylan would, indeed, be furious. Add to that fire the knowledge that he had a grandchild who could be turned against him at Hunter Manning's whim. . . .

That night, when Hunter reached for her in bed, it was with a strange intentness that silenced the protest Stacy had been about to make before the words left her mouth. There was no arguing with a man in this mood, she realized instinctively as he gathered her against the heat of his body, using his hands in a rough urgency that excited against her will.

"You are as stubborn, independent, and maddening as your father claims," he told her thickly, his hands twined deeply into the red-brown of her hair, his mouth hovering just above hers. "But you are my wife, and I'm going to teach you what that means if it's the last thing I accomplish on this earth!"

Stacy met his determined, promising gaze so close to her own and knew he meant it. My God, her mind whispered tantalizingly, what would this man be like if he channeled that power into loving a woman instead of merely possessing her!

Almost as quickly as it had come, the thought was gone, driven out of her immediate consciousness as his body moved sensuously against hers. Soon she was uttering the small cries of surrender and desire Hunter seemed to crave. And then she was caught up once again in the vortex Hunter created around them when he claimed his wife.

CHAPTER EIGHT

The call from Gary Bowen came with complete unexpectedness the next morning at work. Stacy frankly had never thought to hear from her former boyfriend again. Julia took the call and handed the phone over to her boss with a small, speculative glance. Then she disappeared to help a customer in the large greenhouse.

"Stacy?" Gary's voice sounded quite pleasantly familiar. A man like Hunter could make a woman appreciate a softer, gentler man, she told herself wryly. "I just wanted to call and wish you the best. I hear you're already married."

"Yes, it was a very small wedding," Stacy admitted. "It's nice of you to call and congratulate me."

"We were friends, Stacy," Gary reminded her reproachfully. "I'll be honest and say I had hoped it would turn into something more, but I expect it's my own fault for not moving a little faster," he concluded with a rueful, self-deprecating little laugh. "At any rate, I wanted you to know I really am happy for you. If this is what you want, of course," he added with a hint of meaning.

"Naturally it's what I want," Stacy heard herself say with a touch of spirit. She didn't want the whole world speculating on her wedding the way Leana had! "Why else would I have done it?"

"I'm sorry, Stacy, it's just that it all happened so fast," Gary explained carefully. "I was a bit worried you might have rushed into something without giving it a lot of consideration. . . ."

"I considered it from all angles," Stacy assured him with a small, inner wince. If Gary only knew how little real choice there had been! "I'm—I'm quite content with my—" She broke off, realizing she had been about to say she'd been content with her bargain. "With my marriage," she ended coolly.

"And you'll accept my congratulations, after the way I acted at lunch that day?" Gary demanded with a regretful chuckle.

Stacy thought about telling him that his reaction had been extraordinarily tame, according to Hunter's way of thinking, but decided against it. Gary meant well, and they *had* been friends. "Oh, Gary, don't be ridiculous. . . ."

"What about letting me make up for my bad manners? I'd hate to lose the friendship of another small businessperson! It's good to have someone else to talk to about all the trials and tribulations of the free-enterprise system!" he remarked humorously. "Let me take you to lunch this afternoon."

Stacy thought of how her brother and Hunter had that same need and then forced herself to remember that Hunter, at least, had ulterior motives. And that last thought very nearly made her accept Gary's invitation. Why should she let her husband cut her off from her friendships? She had a right to maintain business associations. . . .

"Gary, I'm going to be busy today," she heard herself say and knew she was taking the cowardly way out. But somehow it seemed safer not to risk antagonizing Hunter

158

at this point. She remembered his purposeful manner at breakfast and the way his foggy eyes had followed her as she had gotten ready for work. She wasn't certain what he had been thinking, but it hadn't boded well. A small incident such as that which might be touched off if he found out she'd had lunch with Gary could blow up into something very dangerous, given her husband's present mood.

"Some other time perhaps?" Gary pressed hopefully.

"We'll see," Stacy said hesitantly, growing ruefully more certain by the moment that the risk would be too great. Besides, she reminded herself, Hunter seemed to be honoring his word about not encouraging Leana. Staying clear of Gary was only fair on Stacy's part. "But I'm pretty swamped these days," she added to Gary in a decisive tone that said it all.

"I understand." He sighed. "Well, take care, Stacy, and once again, I wish you the best. If you ever need anything or want a sympathetic ear, keep me in mind, will you?"

"Thank you," she whispered, abruptly grateful for the gesture. Gary was being very kind about all this.

She had barely hung up the phone when it rang again. She raised the receiver once more and heard a friend's voice. A female friend.

"Stacy, I've heard the news. Let's go out to lunch, and you can tell me all about it! I could hardly believe you'd gotten married, but I'm absolutely delighted for you! I want to know every detail. Can you get away today? My treat!"

"Thanks, Carla," Stacy agreed at once. "I'd love it!" Carla was exactly what she needed, she told herself as she hung up the phone for the second time. A friend who truly would wish her the best and who would be enthusiastic about the marriage.

Two hours later Stacy grabbed her van keys and waved

good-bye to Julia. "I'm going out for lunch today, Julia. Be back about one-thirty or so. Can you handle everything?"

"Of course, Stacy, no problem." But there was a strange look in the young clerk's eyes. A look Stacy didn't hang around to decipher.

"I'll be at the Nature Hut restaurant if you need me," Stacy added, slipping out the door.

Lunch with Carla was balm to Stacy's highly strung nerves. Over colorful salads and the restaurant's elegant vegetarian soup, she began to relax. She was even able to laugh as she and Carla discussed the doings of mutual friends.

"Listen, Stacy," Carla said toward the end of the meal, the curve of her short brown hair bobbing a bit as she leaned forward intently. "Is there anything special you need? I hate buying wedding gifts that wind up sitting on the shelf for forty years!" Her attractive, animated face smiled laughingly.

"Need?" Stacy remembered her husband's well-equipped house and shook her head slightly. "You know how it is when two people with established households marry. They end up with two of everything. I really can't think of anything I need."

Carla sighed. "Then it will have to be something frivolous!"

"Well, if you're really serious about this," Stacy amended, grinning.

"I am!"

"We could use a garden hose," Stacy said, thinking of the courtyard.

"A hose! Good grief! Leave it to you to come up with a suggestion like that. Very well, a hose it will be." Carla glanced at her watch. "I realize you're the boss where you

160

work, but my supervisor is expecting me back on the job pretty soon. I hate to call a halt to lunch, but I think I'd better get going."

"I understand." Stacy smiled. "I can't tell you how much I've enjoyed it. Thanks again."

"My pleasure. And remember, this was my treat!"

Carla paused at the cashier's desk to pay the bill, and Stacy moved on ahead. Her practical leather purse swung from her shoulder as she pushed open the heavy door of the restaurant to confront the Tucson warmth. After the air-conditioned comfort indoors, it was always something of a small shock to confront the desert again.

Stacy stood on the top step of the restaurant entrance, digging idly into her pocket for the van's keys and waiting to say a last good-bye to Carla. She glanced up automatically at the properly restrained roar of an expensive car engine, thinking it sounded somewhat like Hunter's car, and froze in astonishment. It was Hunter's car, she realized in surprise. What in the world was he doing here? He worked across town. He wouldn't have driven all this way for lunch. Especially not for roots and berries, as he termed the vegetarian diet!

"Hunter!" she exclaimed, an uncertain smile on her lips as she descended the steps to greet him. "Don't tell me you've grown addicted to good food . . . !"

Her attempt at a light greeting was cut off as soon as she got a good look at her husband's rugged features.

He was in a fury, she realized with a gasp as he climbed quickly out of the car, slamming the door forcefully behind him and advancing toward her with undisguised intent.

"Where is he, Stacy?" he growled, eating up the short distance between them with grim strides. "Still inside? No matter, I can take care of him as easily there as out here!

And when I've finished with Bowen, it will be your turn! Don't think for one split second you're not going to pay for this bit of foolishness!"

He was almost on her, and the fact that she was in danger finally registered in Stacy's astounded consciousness. Hurriedly she retreated back up the steps of the restaurant. But he moved quickly, taking the treads two at a time and reaching out to grab her painfully by the upper arms. The keys fell from Stacy's hands as she stared helplessly up into her husband's face. Never had he looked more like the devil than he did at this moment!

"Hunter! Please. Listen to me! I'm not here with Gary!" The knowledge that she easily might have been at the restaurant with her former boyfriend but for her cowardliness was enough to make Stacy decide to trust her instincts again in the future. Thank God it wasn't Gary inside paying the bill. The trick now was to calm Hunter down while she explained everything to him. But he gave her no chance.

"The hell you're not," he exploded, giving her a small, fierce shake that sent her hair flying from its topknot. "Julia said he'd phoned and you'd gone out to lunch with him! Don't lie to me on top of everything else, Stacy Manning. It's going to go hard enough with you as it is!"

"Julia said—" Abruptly Stacy realized what had happened. Julia had known Gary had phoned, but she'd never heard the second call, which Stacy had taken. The next thing the clerk knew, Stacy had breezily announced she was going out to lunch. No wonder the younger woman had assumed the luncheon engagement was with Bowen.

"That's right! Julia told me where you were when I called to meet you for lunch myself. Little knowing, of course, that you had other plans! So help me, Stacy, I'm going to teach you that I mean what I say if I have to use

162

a rawhide whip on you!" The gray storm of his eyes washed over her.

It occurred to a now trembling Stacy that she had accidentally found the outer limits of her husband's self-control. If she didn't get the situation explained quickly, she would find herself in very unpleasant waters. The tight lines of Hunter's mouth, the totally threatening gleam of his eyes, and the way his fingers dug into the soft skin of her arm were painfully alarming. He really would beat her this time, she thought dazedly, struggling to put together a coherent explanation before he carried out the punishment here outside the restaurant.

"Hunter, it's not Gary inside. Will you stop yelling long enough to let me explain everything?" she pleaded, green eyes beseeching his understanding.

"I would have thought," he bit out dangerously, "that by now you would have learned not to play games with the devil. You know how to push too far, witch. And now that you've learned how to do that, you're going to find out what happens when you do! But first I'm going to take care of your philosophy-spouting friend. . . ."

"Don't call him that!" Stacy hissed.

"I wouldn't waste any time defending him if I were you," Hunter retorted, bringing his face close to hers. She saw the gray shark that now swam in the depths of his eyes and swallowed in genuine fear. "You're going to need all your energy defending yourself!"

"Stacy?" Carla's uncertain, worried voice came unexpectedly from the door of the restaurant. "What's going on here? Shall I get help?"

"Yes!" Stacy gasped even as her husband straightened to glower at the new arrival on the scene.

"Stay out of this, whoever you are. This is my wife, and

163

I'll handle her as I see fit!" He kept his grip on Stacy, who couldn't move.

"Your wife!" Carla gulped in amazement. "Stacy, is this the man you were telling me about during lunch?"

"This is the one," Stacy said, realizing that Carla was her best chance for cooling off her husband's flaming temper. "The man I told you always made me feel guilty because he never seemed to completely lose his self-control in an argument!" Actually, she hadn't really said that to Carla, but the opportunity was too good to miss.

"Stacy, tell your acquaintance here to get lost," Hunter warned.

"Why should I do that? She just paid for my lunch. A wedding present!"

"What's that supposed to mean?" he snarled, his glance going back to Carla.

"Just what she said, I'm afraid," Carla said softly with just a hint of amusement in her voice. "I called Stacy up this morning and invited her out to lunch. I'd heard she'd been recently married and wanted to know all the fascinating details. Is there something wrong with that? I've heard of jealous husbands before, but I always thought they confined their rages to situations where another man was involved!"

"Can't you tell?" Stacy said bitterly over her shoulder, still held fast in Hunter's hands. "He thinks you're another man!"

"Enough of this!" Hunter barked. "Where's Bowen?" He directed the question as much at Carla as at his wife, but Stacy could sense the new uncertainty in him. Soon she would have this matter straightened out. And, she vowed silently, if Hunter thought that would be the end of it, he had a lot to learn!

"Gary Bowen?" Carla asked in astonishment. "Haven't

seen him since he brought Stacy to my last party. That was weeks ago! You thought she was with Gary today? How interesting! Such a reaction. Poor Gary would be horrified at such a primitive response. He's above that sort of thing, himself, you know." Carla was almost giggling now, and Stacy groaned wryly. It wouldn't be long before the details of this embarrassing little scene had been circulated among all her acquaintances.

"You're telling me it was you and not Bowen who just had lunch with my wife?" Hunter demanded in a low voice, his eyes coming to rest on Stacy's face.

"I'm afraid so," Carla admitted. "See here? I've got the receipt for two meals, and I'm sure we could get the waitress to identify us," she added helpfully.

"Would you like more evidence?" Stacy asked with great hauteur. Now that the crisis was fading, her own anger began to kindle. She glared up at her husband's still-grim features and defied him with her brilliant green eyes.

"It would seem," he said slowly, his eyes drinking in his wife's incensed expression, "that Julia made a mistake. . . ."

"It would seem," Stacy corrected significantly, "that you made a mistake. One hell of a mistake!" Relief that it *had* been an error washed through her. The thought of how close she had come to accepting Gary's invitation was frightening. And it fueled her anger.

Abruptly Hunter released his menacing grip on his wife's arms, nodding with a faintly apologetic inclination of his dark head toward Carla. "I'm sorry to have involved you in this, Miss—" he began formally.

"Carla Fowler, and don't apologize," Carla said cheerfully. "I found it quite fascinating."

"Oh, and so did I," Stacy snapped, rubbing her arms

165

beneath the sleeves of her carnation-flowered shirt while she shot her husband a furious glance through her lashes. "I can't tell you how exciting it is to be the subject of a public scene. Especially after having been married only a few days!" She was surprised and much gratified to see a tinge of red on the devil's high cheekbones. Somehow she hadn't expected to find Hunter Manning capable of being embarrassed.

"Well, I expect I'd better be off or I'll never make it back to work this afternoon," Carla said lightly as Stacy fixed Hunter with a glowering look. "Good-bye, Stacy, and don't worry, I won't forget the garden hose. So nice to meet you, Mr. Manning," she added with a grin. "I'd just finished hearing so much about you from Stacy. All of it to your credit, if you're interested! I'll give you a call when I've got the hose properly wrapped in silver paper and a bow, Stacy." And then she was gone, going gracefully down the steps and climbing into her white compact.

"Guess," Stacy invited in a slow, angry drawl, "what the chief topic of conversation will be at Carla Fowler's office this afternoon!"

Hunter drew a deep breath, and Stacy could see him mentally searching for the words. "Stacy, honey," he began carefully, lifting his fingers to stroke the line of her cheek in a strangely gentle fashion. "I don't know what to say. I was so furious to think you might have been here with Bowen, I couldn't think straight."

"How about starting out with 'I'm sorry'?" she suggested bitterly, twisting away from his touch to bend down and scrabble for her fallen keys. When she straightened, she deliberately stepped out of reach. He made no attempt to approach her, the gray eyes lingering hungrily on her face.

"I'm sorry," he whispered and then spoiled the apology

by adding with a relieved sigh, "I'm also damned grateful!" He shook his head as if clearing away the last of the rage that had clouded his mind. "God, Stacy, I was ready to do murder at the thought of you meeting him again! I was so afraid he would be trying to lure you back, make you regret your bargain."

"You were prepared to kill poor Gary?" Stacy gasped, horrified.

"No," he admitted with a twist of his lips. "I would have contented myself with beating him to a pulp."

"And then use a rawhide whip on me!" she exploded.

Hunter opened his mouth to say something, apparently changed his mind, and said instead, "Stacy, let's go home. We can't talk here, and I want to show you—"

"Of all the nerve!" Stacy yelped, starting down the steps and staying just out of arm's length. "You think you can make up for everything by dragging me home and taking me to bed? Isn't that like a man! Well, I've got news for you, Hunter. I don't feel in the least inclined to make love right now. Quite the opposite, in fact. I'm going back to work. If you want to take the afternoon off and go home, be my guest. You can put through a load of washing while you're there!"

"Stacy, you're upset. . . ." he began, attempting to pacify her, following her as she swept off toward the brightly painted van.

"You're damn right I'm upset," she agreed forcefully, swinging around to confront him in the middle of the parking lot, her hands planted on her hips. "And I'm going to stay upset for a long time. At least as long as it takes this tale to make the rounds of all my friends!" she vowed, the bright sunlight glinting off the deep red highlights in her hair as it danced around her shoulders. "I hope you're pleased with the way your revenge is going,

Hunter Manning. I can guarantee this particular Rylan has never been so humiliated in her life!"

She turned away again before he could say anything, yanking open the van's door and leaping inside. She gave him no chance to stop her, twisting the key savagely and snapping the gas pedal to the floor with such force that the abused vehicle fairly leaped out of the parking lot. She left Hunter standing in the middle of the pavement, a grim, unreadable expression on his hard and arrogant face. Not for the first time since she had encountered the devil, Stacy came very close to crying.

The first thing she saw when she entered the driveway of Hunter's house that evening after work was an unfamiliar, gleaming green sports car sitting smugly near the front door. It was all she needed, Stacy thought sadly, parking the van and trailing toward the entrance. She didn't feel in the least like entertaining guests and with her luck whoever drove that sexy green car was probably a very important business associate of her husband's. The car was brand-new, she noted idly as she unlocked the front door and turned briefly to glance at it. It still wore dealer plates. Well, she would do her best not to be deliberately rude. . . .

There was no mumble of voices deep in conversation to be heard as she opened the door and entered the tiled foyer, however.

"Hunter?" she called uncertainly, not wanting to interrupt if he were in the middle of a business conference. His car had been parked near the green one. "I'm home."

There was the clink of ice against glass from the direction of the kitchen, and a moment later Hunter appeared, lounging in the arched doorway with a drink in his hand. He stared at her across the length of the room. Stacy

168

would have given a great deal to know what he was thinking.

"So I see," he observed in response to her announcement. "Still feel like nailing my hide to the greenhouse wall?" he added wryly.

"If I were you," she told him pointedly, tossing her keys down on the table, "I wouldn't bring up the subject." She shot him a slanting glance. "Who owns that green car in the drive?"

"Nice, isn't it?" he inquired, and she saw something flicker in his eyes as he sipped at his drink.

"Well, yes, it is, but whose is it?" she asked, feeling slightly confused.

"It's yours." He watched her face with coolly remote interest.

"Mine!" she gasped, stunned.

"A wedding gift," he explained patiently, not moving. "And, as it turns out, a token of my apologies."

"A car?" she squeaked. "You bought me a car?" She stared at him.

"The van is okay for work, but I thought you should have something more amusing to run around in," he explained, reaching behind himself to pick up another glass and coming toward her with it. "Here," he said, thrusting the wine into her hand. "Let's go take a look at it."

Stacy hesitated, aware of the barely suppressed excitement in him, and knew she couldn't bring herself to throw cold water on it. After all he had done to her today, she still couldn't bring herself to retaliate by throwing his incredible gift in his face. Helplessly she followed him back outside.

"Beautiful, isn't it?" he demanded, unable to keep his enthusiasm in check now. "Look at the instrumentation," he directed, peering into the car's two-seater interior. "And wait until you see what's under the hood!"

Stacy, who had never in her life cared what was under a hood, tried to stifle a totally unexpected grin and couldn't. "Hunter," she said delicately, obeying his injunction and bending down to glance into the cockpit, "I have the feeling you're going to be the kind of father who buys toy trains for his two-year-old daughter and then plays with them himself!"

As soon as the words left her mouth Stacy could have bitten out her tongue. What on earth had made her say that! But the damage was done. Hunter was already withdrawing from his examination of the front dash and turning to her with a sober, glittering look.

"Yes," he agreed, his eyes never leaving hers. "I probably will be that sort of father."

"The—the car is beautiful," Stacy said hastily, forcing her eyes away from the intent expression in his. "There's just one minor complication. I don't know how to drive a standard shift."

"What?" He looked a little blank, as if she had just declared she didn't speak English.

She shrugged ruefully. "Sorry, but I've always stuck with automatic transmissions. Even the van—" Stacy paused. "They're less complicated." She glanced anxiously at his slightly frowning gray gaze. "Perhaps . . . perhaps you'd like to keep it for yourself?" she suggested.

"Of course not. I bought it for you," he said and then added dismissingly, "Never mind, I'll teach you how to drive it."

"Over my dead body," Stacy said sweetly, meaning every word.

"You don't like the car?" he demanded, shocked, clearly, to the core.

"The car is beautiful, but I'll find someone else to teach me how to drive it. Maybe John or Neal from work. . . ."

"Stacy, I will teach you how to drive it," he grated forcefully. "It's my gift to you, and I'll teach you to use it!"

"I can just see that now," she told him with a grim smile. "You'd be yelling at me and scolding and making my life totally miserable. Not a chance. I can't imagine a more horrid situation than having you giving me driving lessons! Unless," she added reflectively, "it's having you waiting for me outside a restaurant!"

"You're going to bring that up? After I've given you a fantastic car like this?" he asked in utter disbelief.

"Did you think the car was going to make me forget the threats you made this afternoon?" she demanded coolly, green eyes slitting a little as she glanced upward into his suddenly forbidding features. "Is that what this is all about? You think you can make up for that piece of humiliation with an expensive gift?" She wasn't certain exactly what was driving her now. Probably the worries she'd had over what she'd decided were his true methods of revenge. She really didn't want to bring up the incident of the restaurant, but it was the only thing she had on hand to use against him.

"Stacy, I'm not in the mood for any more fireworks," he warned gently, too gently. "I've apologized for what happened at the restaurant. I've told you, Julia thought Bowen had called—" He stopped, obviously seeing the flash of guilt Stacy tried to hide. "He *did* call, didn't he?" Hunter suddenly pounced. He gripped her chin between thumb and forefinger and eyed her narrowly. "Didn't he?"

"Well, yes," she admitted huffily, "but I didn't go out with him. You saw that for yourself!"

"But you thought about it, didn't you?" he growled. "That's why you were so frightened at first at the restaurant. Not because you were guilty, but because you'd almost been guilty!"

"Hunter, that's totally illogical!" Stacy protested.

"Be glad what little common sense you've got came to your aid and made you turn down the date," he told her grimly. "Or you would have been quite right to be thoroughly frightened!"

"Don't threaten me, Hunter," Stacy grated, angered anew. "I've got a right to my friends—"

He dropped his hand from her chin and walked past her to open the hood of the car. "Don't be ridiculous," he advised. "Now, come and look at this engine. . . ."

"Hunter!" Stacy blazed, infuriated by his abrupt disinterest in the subject. "I will not let you dictate my friendships or anything else! It was not part of the bargain!"

He looked up at that and there was a long, tension-filled silence while he studied her furious expression. Stacy knew at once she'd gone much too far. She should never have challenged him like that. But one could hardly back down now . . . could one? Damn her temper!

"You," Hunter finally said with absolute finality, not moving from where he stood at the front of the car, "are my wife. That statement sums up the beginning and the end of our bargain. It also fully describes all the fine print. When are you going to get that through your stubborn, independent, red head?"

Stacy took a deep breath and met his newly chilled eyes. "You can't expect me to cut off my social ties. I want to have some friends left when the time comes that you've had enough of this crazy revenge!"

"But we're not talking about just any friends, are we? We're talking about boyfriends, and if you think I'm going

172

to let you maintain relationships like that, you're out of your little mind. Now, why don't you stop trying to provoke me and show me how appreciative you are of your wedding present?" he concluded on a note that should have sounded cajoling but didn't.

"Do you think you can buy my loyalty?" she snapped, growing more outraged by the moment. It had been a difficult afternoon thinking of the tales Carla was no doubt spreading around, and Hunter, in spite of his words, didn't seem all that apologetic. "Do you think expensive gifts will make up for the way you're ruining my life?"

"I'm well aware that a man doesn't ensure his wife's faithfulness with presents," Hunter declared with the attitude of a man who is on the point of giving up all attempt at reasoning. He closed the hood of the little car with a delicate slam and stood for a moment, regarding his wife's flushed face and the way she was chewing nervously on her lower lip. Her wide green eyes watched him warily in return.

"He ensures that commodity with far more elemental tactics," Hunter concluded, taking a purposeful step toward her.

Stacy panicked and, swiveling on her heel, turned to run toward the the only place that seemed to offer shelter in that moment. A place that belonged to her: the greenhouse. He was going to beat her, she told herself helplessly as she fled across the desert-style landscaping. Why had she ever pushed him like that? But she had her pride, hadn't she? She couldn't let him bully her continuously.

Reaching the opaque plastic door of the greenhouse, Stacy yanked it open and went inside, aware that he was following but not at a run. A brief, worried glance over her shoulder showed Hunter coming after his fleeing wife with a steady, determined stride that somehow seemed more menacing than a violent chase would have been. There was a terrible feeling of inevitability about the way he moved, she thought dismally. It was like being patiently stalked. The devil was closing in on his prey and knew there was no rush.

Stacy slammed the greenhouse door, wishing that there were some way to secure it from the inside, and retreated down the rows of beautiful, exotic plants that hung from the ceiling and filled rows of stages. She couldn't go far and turned at bay at the far end of the plant house, surrounded by the brilliant orchids.

Hunter calmly reached the door and stepped inside, his eyes wandering lazily over the lush greenery and incredible colors before coming to rest on his taut-faced wife.

"You know," he remarked, strolling slowly forward. "With that flowery shirt and your green eyes and dark-red hair, you look a little like one of your own orchids. Colorful, temperamental, and in need of someone to take you in hand to keep you from growing wild."

"Hunter, don't touch me!" Stacy warned bravely, putting out a placating hand in a vague attempt to ward him off.

"But I am going to touch you, Stacy," he murmured softly, almost within reach. "I'm going to show you that I don't use presents to buy my wife's loyalty. . . ." The foggy mist of his eyes flowed over her slender, tense figure and there was a tiny, satisfied twist at one corner of his hard mouth.

"If you think you can beat me and get away with it . . . !" Stacy began furiously.

"Is that what you're expecting? A beating? You still don't know me very well, do you, little witch? But I have a plan to remedy that. . . ." With a suddenness that startled her Hunter took the final step that brought him within reach, lowered his shoulder, and, in an instant, swept her across it.

"Hunter!" Stacy yelped, finding herself unexpectedly gazing down at the bottom of the greenhouse floor, her hair falling forward in a tangled mass. "What the hell do you think you're doing!" Automatically she curled one hand into a small fist and pummeled his back.

Hunter put a stop to the brief attack with a sharp, warning slap on her vulnerable rear.

"Ouch!" she gasped, infuriated at the indignity. "Put me down this instant!"

"You'll have to forgive me," Hunter said calmly, turning carefully so that the wriggling burden over his shoulder wouldn't accidentally be swept against any plants. "There's something about this hothouse environment that brings out the primitive in me!" He began making his way out of the orchid house.

Stacy, realizing he wasn't about to set her back on her feet, resigned herself with gritted teeth to being carried across the backyard over her husband's broad shoulder. She could only be grateful for the fact that none of the neighbors were close enough to have a view of the humiliating scene.

"Hunter, I swear I will never forgive you for whatever you're going to do!" Stacy vowed as he opened the back door of the house and carried her inside.

"Don't go making rash statements, honey," he advised, starting down the hall to the bedroom. A moment later he tossed her down in the center of the bed, where she fell in a tangled heap, her face red from the upside-down position in which she had been carried and from her indignation.

"Of all the arrogant, high-handed, overbearing . . ." she began furiously, sweeping the hair out of her eyes with a

175

violent gesture. The action gave her a clear view of what he was doing. "Don't you dare get undressed!"

"It's easier that way." He grinned laconically, unclasping his belt.

"Hunter!" Stacy sought for some argument to stop him. "We haven't even had dinner! And if you think I'm going to let you make love to me after the way you behaved today . . ."

"Some things are more important than dinner," he informed her coolly, his shirt falling to the floor.

"Well, I won't be treated like this!" Stacy made a leap for the far edge of the bed, but Hunter moved even more quickly, launching himself across the short distance and dragging her back as they both fell into the center of the spread.

Stacy squirmed violently for a few moments while Hunter gently worked at securing her. In a brief span of time she lay helplessly pinned beneath him, glaring up into his determined face.

"What do you think this is going to prove?" she managed as she panted from her struggles. Her red-brown brows came together in a fierce line.

"I'm going to show you how I intend to ensure your loyalty," he growled huskily, his hands already at work stripping off her clothes. "And then I'm going to make you tell me how pleased you are with your wedding gift!"

"Damn it! I will not be manipulated!" Stacy swore, trying desperately to free a hand or a leg but finding his greater weight an impossible barrier to freedom. Nowhere was he hurting her, but she couldn't seem to move an inch in any direction. Her wrists were clamped in one of his hands, his legs trapped hers, and his other hand was methodically going about the task of removing her clothes. In a surprisingly short time Hunter had both of them

naked and his warm, hard body stretched along her softness, making every part of her aware of his intent.

She would not give him the satisfaction of any response,
Stacy promised herself grimly, waiting for the sensuous
assault she knew was coming. It was there in his eyes; the
determination to reduce her once again to that creature
who trembled with fierce longing in his arms. But she
would not react to the excitement he was capable of generating. Not this time! Stacy closed her eyes as if to shut
out the reality of her situation, stiffening her whole body
in an effort to resist the onslaught.

But the assault, when it came, was not the aggressive,
arousing thing she had been expecting. Indeed, she barely
felt the first delicate, sensitive caress as Hunter trailed
light fingers across the small, firm shape of her breast. Still
Stacy waited, eyes squeezed shut, for the gentle touch to
turn demanding.

"You are a delight to hold in my arms, sweet witch,"
Hunter whispered against the skin of her throat as he
barely touched it with his lips. "Warm and soft and strong
enough to hold a man the way I want to be held.
. . ."

The tip of his finger rested ever so tenderly on one
nipple, seeking a response but not commanding it. Stacy
held herself rigidly, wondering what trick he would play
on her. The finger at the peak of her breast began a lazy,
circular motion that gently teased.

"Hunter . . ." Stacy groaned softly, her head turning
from side to side on the pillow. "I won't let you do this
to me! Not this time!" But she could feel her own response
and knew a sense of despair.

"It's all right, little flower witch," he soothed, his lips
moving with incredible lightness down to her nipple,
which had been carefully, temptingly aroused. "You can

give yourself to me. I know how to take care of you. And I need you, honey. Doesn't that mean anything to you? I need you just as your flowers need you. . . ." It was his tongue that now circled her nipple. His hand was gliding down to the curve of her stomach, seeking a slow, gentle path to the softness of her thighs.

"You don't need me, Hunter," Stacy protested pleadingly, aware of how her body was eagerly responding to his slow, sensuous, gentle touch. Perhaps if he had used a more forceful approach, she would have been able to resist longer, but the methods he used now were undermining, subtle, and curiously overwhelming.

"I need you, flower lady," he assured her. "You're so sensitive to the needs of an orchid, can't you feel the heat in me? The fire that only you can quench?" He arched himself carefully against her, and Stacy was made totally aware of the masculine desire that he was keeping tightly leashed. He was playing the role of supplicant tonight, pleading, coaxing, begging passionately for her surrender but not demanding it.

Half distrustfully, not quite knowing what to make of Hunter's restraint and gentleness, Stacy turned her face into his shoulder, seeking shelter. His hand, which had been on the verge of touching the soft skin of her inner thigh, lifted instead to stroke her hair with fingers that, to her surprise, trembled.

"Would you touch me with your sweet passion if I free your hands, flower lady?" he whispered. "I long to feel your fingers on me. Give me that much and I will force nothing from you that you don't wish to surrender. . . ."

Stacy shivered at the husky male pleading in his voice. How could she resist this unexpected gentleness? She didn't answer his question, but her body must have communicated its own response because she suddenly found her hands free and instead of using the opportunity to escape, Stacy wound her arms around his neck with a soft, yielding sigh. After this, she thought sadly, he would know how weak she truly was.

But somehow the knowledge didn't seem terribly important at the moment as he held her more closely, urging her in hoarse, longing whispers to touch him, feel him, learn his need of her. She responded, her nails gliding down the hard, muscled back and around to thrust eagerly through the dark hair of his chest. As if they had a life of their own now that they had been freed, her fingers sought the flat male nipples and began to toy with them until Hunter moaned thickly in answer.

The husky sounds of his need, which seemed to spring from deep in his chest, worked a magic on Stacy, calling on something deeply, primordially feminine. Her legs shifted languidly, unconsciously parting for his touch. When his fingers almost hesitantly traced a light pattern on the sensitive inner thigh, her hips arched in response, seeking more of him.

Slowly, helplessly, Stacy felt herself become the supplicant. There was no thought of teasing him tonight. Instead her body began to offer itself boldly, demandingly, pleadingly. She reacted to his delicate lovemaking as if each new, gentle touch were a hint of rain striking the parched desert floor. Each stroke of his fingers was to be savored, consumed, fought over, and when it ended she could only beg for more.

"I want you so much," Hunter breathed heavily. "But I would take nothing more tonight than you would willingly give. . . ."

"Love me, Hunter," Stacy cried hoarsely. "I want you . . . !"

179

"Do you want your devil of a husband tonight, little one?" he asked, making no move to complete the embrace.

"Not a devil," she heard herself protesting breathlessly, pulling him to her and pleading with her body for him to take her. "You're a man, not a devil!" Her eyes opened to flame with the heat of fine emeralds as she met his glittering gray eyes. In that moment she was determined beyond all else to make her statement a reality. She would see the devil in him destroyed, leaving behind a man.

"If you really don't believe you've married the devil himself, would you be willing to create a child with your husband?" he asked wonderingly. "A little red-headed girl with green eyes to whom I shall give toy trains. . . ."

Stacy watched him through her lashes, feeling more helpless than she ever had in her whole life. He asked that she take the ultimate risk for him, and he asked it at a time when he had deliberately made her most vulnerable. Her father's words in the night letter came back to her: *He'll never be able to love a Rylan.*" And suddenly Stacy knew that before she could answer Hunter's question, she must seek another pact with the devil.

"Would you—" She halted and moistened her lips, feeling the intensity of his waiting gaze as if it were a living thing. "Would you love a little girl with Rylan blood in her?" she whispered.

"I would love my daughter," he said with such passion that Stacy believed him. Hunter did not lie. She had the devil's promise. Had she somehow reached into the future and salvaged a little girl's whole life? She felt a vast, overpowering relief, and her fingers lifted to touch the hard plane of his cheek while she smiled tremulously.

"I think," he murmured, bending his head to take her lips, "that I have my answer." For a long, sensuous moment he explored the sweetness of her mouth, drawing

180

forth her response with the expertise of a fine musician tuning an instrument. But Stacy was already at a pitch of excitement, and she longed for nothing more now than to have him moving fully on her, sweeping her into that marvelous rhythm that gave her the short-lived but powerful sensation of being one with her husband.

"Please, Hunter," she whispered invitingly, her hips curving deliberately, hopefully against him. "Please . . ."

"Do you want me enough, little wife, to forgive me for the humiliation I caused you today?" His fingers curled lightly into the warmth between her legs, and Stacy thought she would faint with desire.

"Oh, yes, Hunter, yes, of course I forgive you," she wailed softly, pitiously, clinging to him.

"And my poor wedding gift?" he urged, his voice dropping to an even lower, huskier note while his lips played delicately with her breast.

"Your gift is beautiful. I love it," Stacy cried, growing desperate. "Thank you so much, but please won't you love me now?"

"Like this?" he queried softly, sliding gently, completely between her legs while showering tiny, fragile kisses over her breasts.

"Yes!" The single word came out in a long drawn hiss of pleasure as Hunter moved with the erotic grace of the devil to satisfy his wife.

The style was different this time, slow and agonizingly suspenseful, driving Stacy to new heights of wonder and abandon. In her urgency and need for the man who had enveloped her with his masculine power, Stacy could do nothing but give herself completely. And Hunter made no secret of his pleasure in the gift.

A long time later Stacy slowly uncurled herself from the

warmth of her husband's side and glanced at the clock. Dinner would be late tonight, she decided ruefully, the recent memories still generating enough heat to bring a blush to her face. But the delay in her mealtime was a small price to pay for what she had learned in her husband's arms this evening. He might not love her, she realized with a pang, but he would love his child and perhaps with that a bond could be forged. . . .

"There's just one other thing," Hunter murmured, fog-shrouded eyes watching his wife from where he lay on the pillow.

"What's that?" She half-smiled, thinking of the concessions he had already wrung from her so sweetly tonight. The man had no scruples at all!

"If I ever did catch you out with an ex-boyfriend," he drawled lazily, "I really would beat you!" The gray eyes glittered with male promise.

"Then I shall have to make certain that the person I hire to teach me how to drive my new car isn't an ex-boyfriend, won't I?" she shot back pertly, scurrying for the bath. She closed the door quickly on his muttered oath.

CHAPTER NINE

"I almost forgot," Hunter announced the next morning as he buttered a warm scone Stacy had just taken from the oven. "We're due at the Adamses' tonight after work." He popped the scone into his mouth and chewed enthusiastically, clearly waiting for the explosion.

"The Adamses' " Stacy repeated, astonished. "I don't even know them. And how could you forget something like that, anyway?" She smeared butter on her own scone and frowned at it.

"I'm sorry, honey," he soothed. "It's a long-standing engagement. One I've had since before we were even married, in fact. In all the, er, excitement lately, I'm afraid I've let it slip my mind," he added somewhat apologetically. "But we won't have to stay long, and your brother and Leana will be there, so it's not as if everyone will be a stranger."

Stacy drew a deep breath and faced him across the table. "A business cocktail party?"

"That's about the size of it. All we have to do is put in an appearance—"

"In my jeans?" she interrupted sweetly, not in the least thrilled at the prospect of having to play the part of an elegant and sophisticated wife for her husband's friends.

"I'm sure you'll find something suitable," he retorted,

grinning as he stood up and came around the table to drop a possessive, husbandly little kiss on her forehead before picking up his briefcase in one hand and the remaining scone in the other. "I'll see you after work, honey," he called around a mouthful as he went hurriedly out the door.

"Coward!" she yelled after him and heard his appreciative laughter as he slammed the door behind him.

For a long moment Stacy sat in solitary splendor, glaring at the closed door. Drop a bombshell like that and run, would he? A small, rueful grin tugged at the corner of her mouth as she finally rose to clear the table and hurry out to the waiting van. As she circled the sexy little green car still waiting patiently in the drive, Stacy told herself she'd find something "suitable" all right. Something that would make her husband think twice before surprising her with little announcements like the one at breakfast.

What Stacy found that afternoon at a small boutique owned by a friend was as sexy and green as the car she had received for a wedding gift. The deceptively simple cut clung to her slender figure, half revealing, half concealing. A border of outrageously exotic flowers around the hem floated at her ankles.

"You don't think it's a little too, well, much, Rhea?" Stacy asked her friend, frowning at the image in the mirror.

"It's absolutely perfect on you," Rhea assured her with a warm smile on her attractive face. "Only a slender, supple figure like yours could wear it, and there's something just right about those flowers. Maybe it's just that I've sold you so many flowered shirts, I can't imagine you in any other design!"

"This is something of a switch, isn't it?" Stacy sighed, pulling at the neckline, which plunged from a standup collar that framed her throat to a rather low point. "It's not me at all. . . ."

"Of course it is!" Rhea retorted. "It's just another aspect of you than the one you're accustomed to seeing. Now, if I might make a suggestion about your hair? . . ."

That evening Stacy paced the floor in her high-heeled sandals and green gown, waiting for her husband to come home. She paused more than once to check her appearance in the heavy mirror over the fireplace, her fingers going again and again to the brilliant orchid that nestled in the sleekly drawn knot of hair at the nape of her neck. Under Rhea's prompting, Stacy had temporarily forsaken the casually perched bundle on top of her head in favor of the more severe line. The effect was to focus attention on her green eyes, which now seemed to fill her face. The overall impression was not one of great beauty—Stacy certainly hadn't expected to achieve that miracle—but there was a certain striking quality that caught the eye. Perhaps, she decided, reaching for a shawl as she heard Hunter's car in the drive, it was only her own eye that was caught by the novelty of seeing herself like this.

But there was a difference, and it was something more than only her eye could discern, she realized a moment later as Hunter walked in the door and came to an immediate halt, gray eyes scanning her figure.

"Good lord!" He suddenly grinned as she clutched the shawl tightly in front of her, waiting for his reaction. "I expected something more than jeans but this . . . !"

"You don't like it?" she pounced at once, a little crushed at his response.

"You look very exotic," he assured her, seeing the wariness in her eyes. "I'm not sure it's wise for me to take you outdoors, though. I have a feeling I shall spend the eve-

185

ning fending off men who have suddenly developed an interest in orchids!"

Stacy relaxed and permitted herself a small smile.

"Give me fifteen minutes and I'll be ready," he promised, stepping close to touch her lips briefly with his own before moving toward the bedroom. "We'll take your car," he added as he disappeared down the hall, pulling at his tie. "I want to make sure everything's in good shape."

"Playing with my toys, Hunter?" she mocked lightly.

"Don't tell me you're not the sharing type?" he called back.

Fourteen minutes later he reappeared in a dark suit that seemed to emphasize the formidable appearance he always presented. The equally dark hair with its slash of silver was combed damply back and, as usual, he wore the starkness of white against his tanned skin. Stacy felt her throat constrict with the force of his attraction for her as he escorted her out to the new car and gently helped her into the passenger side.

"Now, pay attention," he instructed, eagerly twisting the key in the ignition. "You can consider this your first lesson." He tossed her a wicked smile and put the car in gear with casual expertise.

"Call it what you like," she said, chuckling. "I'm still not hiring you for an instructor."

But it was a beautifully behaved little car, and Hunter was full of praise for it as they parked in front of the Adamses' lovely foothill home. Stacy felt as if he were making her a gift of his prize mare and had to smile as he carefully locked the door and guided her up the steps of the house.

The party began surprisingly well. The arrival of Hunter's new and unknown wife caused a small but pleasant

186

stir, and Stacy could have sworn there was an element of pure male pride in the way her husband made introductions. Gradually she began to relax, and when Eric and Leana arrived, things promised to become even easier.

But they didn't. Stacy knew the moment she saw her brother and his wife that they had been quarreling again. Or at least Leana had been quarreling. Eric would have been trying to soothe her, Stacy felt sure. It occurred to her that by marrying Hunter, she might have done nothing at all to help her brother's marriage. The knowledge was violently depressing.

"Here, honey," Hunter said at her elbow as Eric and Leana greeted her and moved off to join others. "Let me take that shawl and give it to someone to hang up for you. It's getting warm in here." He started to smile as she obediently allowed him to ease off the silky material, and then his eyes for the first time saw the depth of the neckline on the stunning green dress. The smile changed at once into an ominous frown.

"My God!" he growled. "How dare you appear in public dressed like that?"

"Up until a few seconds ago you liked it," she reminded him cheekily, her mind still on Leana and Eric.

"No wonder you've been clutching that shawl. Well, you can damn well continue to wear it—" He paused, realizing her attention wasn't completely on the lecture she was receiving. "What's wrong, Stacy?" he asked in an entirely different tone.

"Oh, Hunter," she sighed morosely. "It's Eric and Leana. Every time I see them things seem to be getting worse."

Hunter shot a swift, considering glance toward the other couple and at that moment Leana looked up and saw his attention. She smiled at him from across the room, a

187

warm, intimate smile that made Stacy's blood run very cold. Hunter looked back at his wife, a new frown on his harsh features.

"You have a marriage of your own to worry about. Let Eric and Leana work out their problems by themselves."

Stacy shook her head sadly, taking a sip of the white wine in her glass. "I don't know, Hunter, I just don't know."

"Well, I know I'm not going to let you brood about someone else's problems tonight," he informed her gruffly, taking her by the arm. "Come over to the hors d'oeuvre table and tell me which ones I can eat!"

There ensued several moments of entertainment at the laden table while Hunter regaled everyone present with his trials and tribulations as an enforced vegetarian. Stacy flushed a light pink as he teased her lightly, affectionately in front of the others.

"But what do you eat?" one middle-aged lady inquired, blue eyes alight with genuine interest as she glanced at Stacy.

"Roots and berries," Hunter answered at once, grinning down at his wife.

"Seriously." The woman smiled, and Stacy, realizing the question was an honest one, began to talk about her personal decision to avoid meat.

"But can you get enough protein?" the lady asked and several others in the group waited interestedly for the answer.

"Oh, yes." Stacy laughed. "It's a myth that one must have meat to get protein, you know." She launched eagerly into a favorite topic and it was a long time before she realized that Hunter had disappeared from her side.

In fact, she realized it at about the same moment that she glanced up and found another man's eyes on her. She had just finished detailing a recipe for an elegant meatless quiche, which the original questioner had requested. In Stacy's enthusiasm, the shawl had been forgotten. She was leaning over the hors d'oeuvre table, scribbling measurements on a cocktail napkin, and it was as she straightened that she realized Hunter was gone and she had become the focal point of a good-looking, sandy-haired young man. His interested brown gaze went from the low point of her now-exposed neckline up to her face, and then he smiled quite deliberately.

"Your eyes match your dress," he observed in a low tone as the others around them drifted off. "Very effective." The words were accompanied by a surprisingly intense look that Stacy found disconcerting.

"Thank you," she managed formally, not knowing what else to say, and turned to move away.

"I'm Anthony Hogan, by the way," the stranger added quickly. "And I just arrived. Hardly know a soul, and I gather you're in the same boat?"

"Not quite. My brother and his wife are here. Also my husband," Stacy responded with a polite smile. "I'm Stacy Manning." Funny how the name came automatically. She had only been married a few days.

"I heard you talking about your diet," Anthony went on glibly. "I've always been interested in health foods and"—his eyes shifted briefly to her hair—"orchids."

"Really?" Stacy felt herself warming up to this handsome young man. "I grow them, you know," she confided eagerly. "Mostly as a hobby, but it goes along with my business."

"What would that be?" Anthony invited, politely reaching out to take her empty wineglass and filling it from a bottle near the buffet table.

"I own a nursery," Stacy told him.

He laughed. "What a pleasant change from the boutiques women in your class usually run. When they work at all, that is."

"What do you mean, women like me?" Stacy demanded, a small frown appearing on her forehead.

Anthony shrugged. "The wives of successful men usually seem to just dabble at things when they work. It's rare to find one who's got an honest job."

Stacy decided he was trying to compliment her. "What about yourself, Mr. Hogan?" She wondered where her husband was. There was no sign of him.

"Call me Anthony," he said, smiling. "And, yes, I work for a living, too. My firm recently moved me here from California."

"And how long have you been interested in orchids?" Stacy asked, sipping at the wine he had poured and wondering if she should go searching for Hunter.

"Probably for about ten minutes," drawled a familiar, deep voice full of lazy warning from directly behind her.

"Hunter!" she exclaimed. "I was wondering where you'd gone. . . ."

"I had a little business to attend to." He smiled coolly. His slightly chilled, foglike gaze was on Anthony Hogan. Stacy made introductions quickly, not quite certain of Hunter's temper. Both men shook hands stiffly, their eyes meeting in a man-to-man look that left Stacy out entirely. She only knew that when it was finished, Anthony made an excuse and took himself off into the crowd.

"Good heavens, Hunter," she exclaimed, somewhat annoyed. "I think you frightened him!"

"Perhaps I should work a little more on techniques for frightening my wife," he remarked laconically, taking her arm. "I thought I told you to keep that shawl around you!"

Stacy glanced down at where the shawl hung loosely, no longer covering the opening of the dress. "You told me to wear something appropriate." She grinned daringly.

"Next time," he vowed ominously, "I'll accompany you when you go shopping! Let's go, honey, we've done our duty. Make your good-byes."

"We're leaving already?" she asked, surprised.

"I told you we were only going to put in an appearance. I consider myself still on my honeymoon, and I have better things to do with my time."

"Oh." Stacy hid her small flush by glancing around expectantly. "Where are Eric and Leana? I'll say good-bye to them first."

"Eric and Leana," Hunter announced with satisfaction, "have already left."

"What? I didn't see them go!"

"They left by the back door. Didn't want to cause a commotion, I expect."

"Hunter, what have you been up to?" Stacy demanded, swinging around to confront him suspiciously. "What do you mean, they've already left? Leana loves parties like this. She wouldn't be willing to go home so early."

"I'm not at all certain she was willing," Hunter told her with a quirking smile. "That's why Eric took her out by the back door."

"Hunter!" Stacy thought she would scream in exasperation. "What's going on?"

"Your brother is an intelligent man," Hunter told her calmly. "I gave him a little advice, which, when the opportunity arose, he seemed inclined to follow. If my hunch is right, you won't need to be so concerned about that marriage. . . ."

"What advice? What opportunity? Hunter, if you don't tell me what you've done, I'll—" Stacy broke off, appalled

191

at a sudden thought. "Oh, no! You didn't—you didn't tell Eric to beat Leana, did you?" She stared up at him, green eyes filled with horror.

"Come on, let's go home and I'll tell you all the gory details." Hunter grinned.

Fifteen minutes later Hunter guided the beautiful green car out of the drive and started down the street. Stacy whirled to confront his profile.

"Now tell me exactly what happened!" she ordered.

"Well, the long and the short of it is, I told Eric his wife was turning into a flirt and that if she met with disaster, it was going to be all his fault," Hunter began calmly.

"*His* fault!" Stacy was almost speechless.

"Precisely. I let him know that a beautiful, young, high-spirited woman like Leana needs to have the boundary lines drawn very sharply. I told him he wasn't doing the marriage any favors by letting her get out of hand."

"Oh, my God!" Stacy sank back into the bucket seat with a groan.

"Then, to prove to Eric that Leana was, indeed, in danger, I set her up."

"Hunter, how could you!" Stacy hissed, shaking her head helplessly.

"It was simple, really," he explained kindly. "I merely invited Leana out onto the terrace by the pool to tell me how life was treating her these days. She needed no further encouragement. She began a sorrowful tale of how Eric didn't understand her and how she had thought I did. When she threw herself, crying beautifully, into my arms, Eric stepped out of the shadows and took over."

Stacy ground her teeth. "Of all the sneaky, underhanded, conniving tricks! Poor Leana!"

"Poor Leana is, with any luck, getting exactly what she deserves right now. Watching his wife throw herself into another man's arms was a little too much, even for the patient Eric."

"You idiot! Eric will hate you for this!" Stacy sighed.

"No, he won't. He's been going through hell lately, Stacy. I know, I've talked to him on a couple of occasions. Tonight when he learns he can control his wife as well as Rylan Enterprises, he's going to be very grateful."

"Grateful to you," Stacy said with sudden perception, "because you've let him know it's okay to do both using different techniques than my father did." She paused a moment and then said softly, "But what happens if Leana tells Eric that at one time you really were encouraging her?"

"I, uh, took the opportunity of the few minutes I had on the terrace to inform Leana that she had completely misread my earlier attentions; that I had felt sorry for her but now realized she had a husband who loved her and that she didn't really need a confidant. Eric overheard that, and he'll see anything she tells him in that light. Especially since I've already made it clear to him that my sole female interest is my own wife."

"And he believed you?" Stacy asked a trifle distantly, not looking at him.

"Of course. Besides, I doubt that Leana is going to try incriminating me anyhow. The only way she can do it is by incriminating herself," Hunter noted, not without satisfaction.

"I saw you kiss her on the patio that first night at my brother's house," Stacy said quietly.

"That peck on the nose? Believe it or not, that was the only time I'd done so and it hardly qualified as a lover's caress!"

"So you've neatly arranged to cast blame on no one but Leana—"

"And on Eric!"

"Still, it's Leana who's going to suffer," Stacy groaned.

"She isn't the only one suffering," Hunter shot back, sounding a bit miffed that Stacy didn't see the full perfection of his plan.

"What do you mean?"

"Never mind," he growled. "But if it makes you feel any better, the beating I told Eric to administer was only part of the prescription. I told him that when that was finished he should take her to bed!"

"And my brother is planning on taking all this grand advice?" Stacy asked scornfully, wondering how men could be so dumb.

"Just as if he'd gotten it from an older, wiser, and more experienced brother," Hunter assured her coolly. "He trusts me."

Stacy waited a full minute, staring thoughtfully out the window before asking the chief question on her mind.

"Why, Hunter?"

"Why does he trust me?"

"No. Why are you attempting in your own inimitable style to save my brother's marriage?" Stacy couldn't bring herself to meet the glance he tossed at her from the other side of the car. As crazy as she privately thought Hunter's approach was, she didn't doubt for a moment that it was a genuine attempt to help. And she wondered why. Once again it occurred to her that a grateful Eric represented a potent weapon that Hunter could use against Paul J. Rylan.

"I like your brother," Hunter said quietly. "Let's let it go at that."

Under the circumstances it was understandable that the next morning when Julia told Stacy her brother was on the

194

phone, she took the call with a certain amount of dread. Would Eric be calling to tell her his marriage was in ruins?

"Hi, Stacy," he began on a cheerful note that astonished her. She hadn't heard him sound that carefree in weeks. "I'm calling to give you the word from on high."

"What do you mean?" she demanded, frowning into the phone and wondering what was going on.

"Just had a call from Dad. He's going to be arriving back in Tucson tomorrow. Spoke briefly to Mom, too. She wanted to know all about Hunter, naturally." Eric laughed. "So I gave her a complete rundown. She's a fan for life."

"Why should that be?" Stacy asked, astonished. "She hasn't even met him!" Or had her mother remembered that twenty-year-old who had come pleading?

"Ah, but you forget!" Eric advised her wisely. "Hunter's got everything she's ever wanted in a husband for you. He's successful, he's socially accepted, and he's gotten you into a dress on more than one occasion. I told her about that green thing last night. She can't wait to see you looking all dressed up. It's something she was never able to accomplish, so she figures he must have some kind of special power."

"The only thing he did was tell me to find something suitable," Stacy announced haughtily. "I did the rest!"

"Because you didn't want to embarrass him?"

"Eric!" She hadn't wanted to embarrass herself!

"It's okay, Sister dear. We all do some strange things for the people we love. Speaking of which, tell your husband he was absolutely right."

"About what?"

"He'll know. You can add that for the first time in weeks I am a happily married man!" With a wholly male chuckle Eric hung up the phone.

That night Hunter eyed Stacy thoughtfully when she appeared from the kitchen carrying a vegetable casserole that was plunked down onto the table with undue force.

"Something wrong?" he inquired dryly, helping himself to the delicious-smelling vegetable and cheese mixture.

"My mother and father will be home tomorrow," she told him tightly.

"And this is the reason you've been stomping around the house ever since I got home from work?" he pressed blandly, reaching for a whole wheat roll.

"They'll be out here to meet you, Hunter, as soon as possible. I know they will," Stacy said, chewing on her lower lip as she took the chair opposite her husband.

"So?"

"They're coming home much earlier than planned, Hunter," she explained carefully. "Who knows what my father's going to do?" She stared at him worriedly, wondering how he could look so bland at the prospect of seeing Paul J. Rylan.

"Whatever happens, your father and I will, I'm sure, conduct ourselves like gentlemen. There's no need to look so concerned," Hunter commented.

Stacy drew in a deep breath, wishing the coming confrontation between the two men could be postponed. Now, why should she want that? she asked herself. The arrival of her father represented the appearance of her one potential ally. Paul J. was the one member of the family who might be smart enough and ruthless enough to find a way out of this situation. . . .

Something in her husband's foggy eyes hardened as he watched the play of emotions across her face. "You will not, I trust, forget to which family you now belong," he drawled in warning, one black brow elevated quellingly.

"Regardless of what happens when I again meet your father, you are still my wife, Stacy."

"And will you remember the terms of our bargain?" Stacy flung back, annoyed at the feeling of guilt she was experiencing when she contemplated a solution to the dilemma in which she found herself. "This marriage was sole and complete payment."

"I always keep my bargains," he told her evenly. "And now that you're a Manning, you will want to uphold that family tradition, I'm sure!"

CHAPTER TEN

The confrontation came with unnerving swiftness, at least as far as Stacy was concerned. The time and place were established the next morning when a rather subdued-sounding Leana called Stacy to invite Hunter and his new wife for a small welcome-back party for the Rylans.

"Just a few friends of theirs and family, of course, Stacy. Why don't you wear something nice like that green thing you wore the other night. Your mother will be thrilled to see you looking so sophisticated!" Leana chuckled, the humor sounding genuine. "It will be the perfect opportunity to introduce your parents to their new son-in-law. Seven o'clock all right?"

Might as well get it over, Stacy thought with her usual wish to get the worst out of the way. "We'll be there, Leana." A moment later she picked up the phone and dialed Hunter at his office to tell him the news.

He listened and agreed to the appointment with a quietness in his voice that told her nothing of what he was thinking. "Still worried, Stacy?" he asked coolly.

"I hate scenes," she told him grimly.

"I certainly don't intend to cause one, and I somehow don't think your father will, either. At least, not in front of others," he amended. "Planning to go in your jeans?"

Stacy frowned at the suspicion of humor in his words. "Would you mind if I did?" she asked scornfully.

"Yes," he retorted, sounding thoughtful. "I think I would this time. You'll feel better if you're dressed as well as the others will be."

"Does it matter how I feel?" she chided, thinking that all Hunter probably had on his mind was showing her father how much a Manning bride she now was.

"Yes, Stacy, it matters. Oh, and, Stacy," he added, as she would have hung up the phone. "Find something else besides that green thing. Something with a higher neckline."

The dress Stacy found, with the assistance of her friend who owned the boutique, was as high-necklined as Hunter could have wished. It was also long-sleeved. Made out of black silk, it was cut so severely as to seem austere. Only the startling splash of orchids scattered about from hem to neck relieved the overly stark impression. The orchids were handpainted on the material and the dress cost a fortune.

That night when Stacy swept into the small cocktail party on Hunter's arm, she was fiercely glad she'd spent the money. The right clothes in the right environment could relieve a certain amount of anxiety, she discovered. She didn't notice, although everyone else present did, that the cool sophistication of the black dress, together with her sleekly bound hair, made her a perfect mate for the man at her side. Stacy only knew that she found herself holding onto Hunter's arm with more than necessary strength as Miriam Rylan rushed forward.

"Stacy, darling, you look fabulous! It's so good to see you again!" Miriam, sleek and fashionable in her middle years, hugged her daughter with casual maternal attention. It was obvious her main interest was the man standing beside her daughter. "I just had to come home and see your husband!

"And you, of course, are Hunter. The one responsible for saving my daughter from marrying that philosophy type who runs a bookstore!" she chuckled, taking Hunter's hand and lifting her face for a gracious kiss on the cheek. To Stacy's surprise, Hunter granted the small caress and followed up with a smile for his mother-in-law. Miriam's beautifully made-up eyes twinkled delightedly, and she tilted her pert head with its deceptively casual short blond hair to one side.

"I'm Hunter," Stacy's husband murmured politely. "And I'm afraid the philosophy type really didn't put up much of a fight!"

Miriam laughed. "Do come and meet Paul . . ." she began, only to be interrupted by a cool, gruff voice behind her.

"Hello, Manning," Paul J. Rylan said calmly, his piercing blue eyes going first from his daughter's frozen expression to Hunter's even more remote look. "How interesting that we should meet again after all these years."

"Darling, do you know Hunter?" Miriam exclaimed in astonishment. She turned to glance at her still trim and attractive husband. The light gleamed on the deep redbrown of his admittedly thinning hair and, although he had the blue eyes he had bequeathed his son, there was something in the arrogant slant of his cheek line and in the forceful chin that somehow put a disinterested observer in mind of his daughter.

"Hunter and I met briefly several years ago," Paul told his wife, not glancing at her. His whole attention was on Hunter.

"How ever did that come about?" Miriam asked in interested amusement.

"It was a matter of business," Hunter told her, his gray eyes foggier and more unreadable than Stacy had ever seen them. She shivered but did not loosen her hold on his arm.

"How fascinating." Miriam smiled, clearly not remembering the incident at all. Perhaps in time she would begin to wonder about that odd silver slash in Hunter's dark hair, Stacy thought, but not tonight.

It was just as Hunter had predicted, Stacy thought wonderingly a few minutes later as Leana pressed a cool glass of wine into her hand and made introductions to the other guests present. No scenes. At least not in front of the others. For the first time in her life Stacy had cause to thank the dictates of good manners that provided a breathing space for her to react with some semblance of normality. Hunter stayed close by her side, the perfect, attentive husband, and the conversation quickly flowed into a discussion of the Rylans' recent trip. Stacy let the others carry on the discussion, grateful for this curious interlude. She was sipping quietly at her wine when she happened to glance up and catch Leana smiling across the room at Eric, who responded at once. It had been a long time since her sister-in-law had looked at Eric like that, Stacy told herself and wondered how Hunter's ridiculous plan could ever have worked. But the evidence certainly indicated that it had been successful. She smiled wryly to herself. Hunter was having an equal amount of success charming her mother. Miriam made it clear she couldn't have been more pleased with him. After having given up on her daughter doing the right thing years ago, the marriage to Hunter must have been a vast relief to her.

It was twenty minutes later when Paul Rylan approached his daughter with a polite, cool smile and asked if she and Hunter would care to accompany him out on the patio. Stacy glanced involuntarily at her husband, who simply took her arm and started forward.

"Of course, we'll go outside with you for a while, Paul," Hunter said with such distant politeness that Stacy didn't know what to think. Both men seemed suddenly intent on finding an isolated place, she realized. It was as if, by some unspoken but mutual agreement, they had decided the time for a showdown had come. And she would be the one in the middle.

It was somehow fitting that the patio, the place where she had first encountered Hunter, should be the scene for this confrontation, Stacy thought grimly as she walked between the two men out the sliding glass doors and into the cool, shadowy area at the back of the house. It even smelled the same out here as it had that night, she thought in strange wonder. Had it really been such a short time ago?

Her father wasted no time. Once they were alone he turned to face Stacy and Hunter, his eyes going first to his daughter's pale, taut features.

"You know what this is all about, of course?" he inquired calmly, idly swirling the contents of the glass in his hand.

"Yes," Stacy replied equally calmly, not knowing where she was drawing the strength unless it was from Hunter, whose arm she still held.

"She's known from the beginning," Hunter said flatly. "She stood near where you're standing now and made a bargain with me, Rylan."

"Why would she do that?" Paul Rylan inquired casually. "The one thing about you that I have never questioned, Stacy, is your intelligence."

"She did it," Hunter said with chilling politeness, "to pay off the Rylan debt."

"I see. That business with your father." Paul sipped his drink. There was a long and tension-filled pause and then he remarked quietly, "It wasn't necessary, Stacy. I would have dealt with the matter." His blue eyes flickered in the shadowy light.

"You weren't here to handle it," Stacy told him evenly. "There were only Eric and Leana. . . ."

"Ah," Paul said softly, thoughtfully, nodding his head. "I begin to understand. I won't ask how you intended to threaten my son, Manning, I'd rather not know. Can I assume Stacy demanded to pay the debt in place of her brother?"

The two men watched each other with cold, unnerving expressions. "Something like that," Hunter finally allowed almost gently.

"Do Eric and Leana know?" Paul asked.

"No."

"Thank you," Paul said surprisingly.

"Don't thank me, thank Stacy," Hunter retorted.

"Yes," the older man nodded. "My reckless, wayward, stubborn daughter. You're no fool, Stacy. I figured you probably knew what you were doing. The only reason we're home early is because your mother couldn't bear the suspense of wondering what kind of man you'd married. I knew you were capable of looking after yourself, of course."

"She may be capable of it, but she won't need to do so unassisted any longer," Hunter interposed smoothly. "She's a Manning now, Rylan. My wife. I will look after her."

Stacy slanted a curious sideways glance at her husband, not understanding the intensity of his words.

Paul Rylan ignored Hunter and spoke directly to his daughter. "You apparently went into this with your eyes

203

open, girl. Don't get any false notions now. This matter of his having made a lifelong friend out of Eric and the way he is bent on meeting all your mother's hopes for a son-in-law, they are only ways of consolidating his revenge, Stacy. I did some checking on your husband yesterday. The boy of fourteen years ago has become a man with a vengeance. He's smart and he's extraordinarily thorough. Anyone he's done business with will tell you that. He knows how to sew up a deal—"

"If you checked that thoroughly," Stacy interrupted with great assurance, "then you must know my husband is a man of his word. I have his promise that I am payment in full for what you did to his father."

"You believe that? You don't think he has ulterior motives for gaining Eric's confidence and for winning over your mother?" Paul asked with faintly amused scorn.

"I worried about it at first, the same way I worried when he told me he wanted a child. . . ." Her father's face tightened, and she knew he had just realized the full potential of the marriage for revenge. Stacy was now painfully aware of Hunter's eyes on her profile. She drew a deep breath and continued. "But I have his word that he would love his child, and that means he would never use her as a weapon. I also have my husband's word that he made friends with Eric because he happens to like him. It's as simple as that." She felt Hunter stiffen but did not turn to glance at him.

"You believe all this?" her father asked again.

"Yes," Stacy said simply. "I believe it."

Paul Rylan stared at her for a moment longer and then he inclined his head with an air of decision. He turned to face Hunter.

"My daughter has taken it upon herself to make up for what happened fourteen years ago, Manning. Yes, I admit something was owed. Your father was a bull-headed, stubborn, uncompromising man. He was a lot like me. We could never have worked together, and he would have been the first to tell you that. Still, I have looked back once or twice since that business deal and thought that perhaps things could have been handled differently. . . . But it's over now. There's no going back for any of us. I will let you have my daughter as payment, partly because there's nothing I can do to prevent it." Rylan's mouth quirked upward ruefully. "I never could do much with her! And partly because I think you will one day discover that she has as much courage and determination as either you or I. She seems to have combined it with a woman's faith in her man, and that, my boy, is a tough combination to beat. You may have made a Manning out of her, but she's also my daughter. You and I will be quite helpless when she fully realizes her own power. I'm very much afraid that the weapon you have used against me will ultimately prove a chain that will tie the Rylans and the Mannings together."

Paul leaned forward and dropped a small, paternal kiss on his daughter's forehead. Then he stepped back with a small, very private smile and turned to walk indoors.

Stacy stood very still, watching her father disappear into the house, her emotions vibrating to the tension of the moment. She realized vaguely that she was still gripping Hunter's arm, but she couldn't bring herself to meet the cloudy pools of his eyes. She knew he was watching her, though, and she sensed that something besides anger or scorn was making him tense. She could feel that tension in him as if it were physically radiating outward. He seemed almost wary. Wary? Hunter? That didn't make sense.

Hunter shifted slightly, and when he spoke, his words were not at all what Stacy had expected to hear.

"You may consider the debt paid." His tone was low, enigmatic, and it made Stacy turn to face him at last, her hand falling from his sleeve.

"What?" she whispered, frowning up at his harshly carved features. In the dim light of the patio he looked more like a dark devil than ever. The flash of silver in his hair gleamed as if it were moonlight on water.

"Your father was right, Stacy," he told her heavily, his expression remote and very, very distant. The gray eyes were bleak beyond description. "There is no going back to adjust the past. And it does no good to drag others down in an attempt to do so."

"Hunter, I don't understand," she murmured helplessly, fearing something new and dangerous.

He stared down into her upturned face for a long while, searching for she knew not what. "You told me once I couldn't have both happiness and revenge; that I must choose. I don't know yet if I'll find the happiness, but I'm certain I don't want the revenge. The kind of ruthlessness it takes to go after it breeds men like your father. Like my father. Hard, cold men who, even if they respect them, can't communicate with their own children. I have been learning lately that I want something else out of life. I don't want to end up like either of our fathers. It's as simple as that." He took a breath. "So I'm setting you free. Wiping out the debt."

For an instant Stacy was utterly speechless under the force of a sudden, overwhelming fury. It swept her from head to toe, and it took several seconds before she could manage to declare in a voice that shook with anger, "Like hell it's that simple! If you think you can come into my life, turn it upside down, and then walk out again, you can damn well think again. You have a wife now, Hunter Manning, and one of these days you'll have a daughter and perhaps a son. You may have married for revenge, but one way or another you're stuck with that marriage. You've got responsibilities!"

Something flickered to life in Hunter's cold, foggy eyes, something new and warm, but Stacy didn't pause. She was too wound up, too emotionally charged to do more than draw breath before continuing with her tirade.

"You just heard me give my father lecture number fifty-eight on the subject of how your word is your bond. Are you going to make a liar out of me? You swore once, in front of witnesses, to love and cherish till death us do part. I realize you probably had your fingers crossed when you vowed to love me, but surely a *Manning* would have too much pride to turn his back on all the other promises!" Once again she paused for a split second to gather her anger and her breath, and in that short space Hunter spoke.

"I didn't, Stacy," he said with an incredible gentleness. That which had flickered alive in his eyes was beginning to glow now, although his face was still a harsh landscape in the moonlight.

Stacy glowered at him. "You didn't what?" she demanded.

"I didn't have my fingers crossed during the part where I promised to love. Did you?" Hunter put out his large hands and framed her shadow-etched features, his eyes sweeping her face with a curious expression that she might, if she were feeling very optimistic, have labeled hope.

"No," she breathed in a small, amazed whisper. "No, Hunter, I forgot to cross my fingers during that part."

"Stacy," he said with great caution, as if he were almost

afraid to ask, "do you think that perhaps someday you could do more than develop faith in my word of honor? Do you think," he grated, "you could learn to love the devil?"

"Does the devil want love?" she murmured, an overpowering sense of happiness warming every inch of her, the emeralds in her eyes coming alive with heat.

"The devil in me—" He hesitated. "No, the man in me wants your love very, very much, Stacy, my little flower lady."

"Can—" She swallowed tightly, hardly daring to hope. "Can the man in you give as well as receive love?"

"The man in me has wanted you, I think, from the first night when you stood out here on the patio and defied me so bravely, lecturing me about the futility of revenge and finally bargaining with the devil. I'm not sure when the want turned to love. I only know that from the beginning I wanted to take no chances on losing you. I told myself then that the reason I was insisting on marriage was to deepen the revenge, but I know now that it was just an instinctive reaction. I wanted to create all sorts of chains with which to bind you. I wanted that warmth and spirit and strength to belong only to me. . . ."

"Oh, Hunter . . ."

"You were wrong when you told your father I had no ulterior motives in befriending Eric or in making a good impression on your mother or in wanting you to have my child. I did all three because I saw them as ways to hold you," Hunter confessed, and she could feel the slight trembling in his fingers, which still framed her face. "Can you forgive all that and let me try to make you happy?"

"No." She smiled and for the first time since she was a very young girl, Stacy felt actual moisture behind her eyes. "No, Hunter, I can't forget that. I shall *treasure* all that!

208

I love you. In the beginning I told myself I was only marrying for my family's sake, but you were right that first night when you told me I'm not made of martyr material. Something in me recognized something in you and wanted it, needed it. There is a strength in you that has nothing to do with the devil, and a passion and a capacity for gentleness. It was my pride and my natural stubbornness that made me drag my heels all the way. I never really wanted to be free of our bargain."

"Oh, my sweet witch," Hunter breathed, folding her close against his hard warmth. "We came together for all the wrong reasons, but if that was the way we were fated to meet, I can't regret any of it. I'm only grateful that that part is behind us now. When you're in my arms, I can only concentrate on the present and the future." Stacy felt a strange moisture on her face. She knew there were tears of her own on her cheeks, but with a feeling of wonder she realized Hunter's were there also.

With a sense of deep love and compassion, Stacy lifted a finger to touch the wetness on his face and smiled tremulously up into the gray mists of his eyes. Mists that shone now with a gentleness she had never seen in them. Stacy realized that neither of them was embarrassed by the tears. For the next few moments there were no words between them, only a communion that spoke volumes. Hunter held his wife with wonder and love and promise.

Eventually Stacy stirred in his arms, lifting her head from his shoulder and smiling. "I suppose we ought to be getting back inside. People will wonder—" The words were barely out of her mouth when Eric's cheerful voice reached them from the sliding glass window.

"Hey there, lovebirds, we're opening the champagne. Want to join the rest of us?"

"What are you going to celebrate with it?" Hunter

joked, wrapping his arm around Stacy's waist and starting reluctantly back toward the party.

"A great deal, I think." Eric smiled and then broke into a chuckle. "A great deal, indeed. You and I are very lucky men, Manning."

"Yes," Hunter agreed softly, glancing down at his wife. "We both seem to have had the devil's own luck recently, haven't we?"

Stacy's green eyes gleamed. She felt she ought to contradict that statement, but she was far too happy to do it just then.

It was a long time later when Hunter and Stacy finally walked through their own front door and the privacy of their home.

"I was beginning to think the evening would never end." Hunter grinned, closing the door and coming up behind his wife to pull her back into his arms.

"You were the model of the perfect new husband." Stacy smiled as his arms came around her waist, and she put her hands on top of his. His breath was warm in her hair.

"I was, wasn't I? I guess it comes naturally," he observed modestly. "But, then, I've been getting in some practice lately. How have you come to feel about the role of wife?"

"Haven't you noticed how well I'm adjusting to it?"

"Let's go practice some more," he suggested with a small groan of urgency. "I want to hear what it sounds like when you tell me you love me while you're lying naked in my arms."

"You think it's going to sound any different than when I stand here fully dressed and tell you?" she teased, turning in his embrace to wind her arms around his waist.

"I'm afraid you've married a very greedy man, flower

witch," he growled softly. "I want to hear it both ways, always. I want to hear it across the breakfast table and while we're listening to Vivaldi and when I call you at work and when I make love to you . . ."

"I shall be just as greedy," she warned gently, lifting her lips invitingly.

"I love you, Stacy Rylan Manning. . . ." he whispered huskily, his mouth hovering above hers.

"I have your word on that?" she demanded lightly.

"My word of honor. I will never go back on the bargain of our marriage." His lips captured hers in a kiss that conveyed the spectrum of his love; the need, the desire, the gentleness, and the power of it.

And Stacy responded with all the warmth and depth of her own love, her arms tightening around him, her body pressing gently, intimately inward toward his heat.

"I was trying very hard to be noble out there on the patio tonight," he abruptly confided, bending to lift her into his arms, "when I said I was setting you free. In reality, I see now I couldn't have done it." He looked down into her glowing face. "I don't know whether or not there is still something of the devil in me, but I know I intend to hold onto my own. I will tend my garden very carefully for the rest of my life," he added in a hoarse murmur, starting down the hall toward the bedroom with a determined stride.

"I told you once that gardens can be very demanding." Stacy smiled, toying with the silver in his hair. "They require a great deal of attention and love. . . ."

"You have it from your father's own lips that I'm nothing if not thorough. I know how to sew up a deal so tightly, none of the parties involved can escape!"

"Hunter," Stacy said suddenly as he set her down beside the bed. "That was very kind of you to shake his hand when we left this evening."

"That wasn't kindness, that was a realization that without him I would never have met you." Hunter smiled down into her loving eyes. "And nothing else in the world matters to me but you."

"Oh, Hunter, my darling Hunter," she breathed, her hands going around his neck. "I love you so much. . . ."

Slowly, with infinite care, Hunter undressed her, letting the black silk dress glide to her feet, where the orchids in the pattern looked like the contents of a scattered bouquet. As if savoring every inch of her, he gently removed the remaining garments and finally the pins holding her hair until she stood naked beneath his hands. Her own fingers, trembling a bit with need and love, undid the whiteness of his shirt and then went to his belt buckle. When they both were undressed, Hunter set Stacy very tenderly on the turned-back bed and lowered himself beside her.

"You're going to bare your little teeth at me and give me a lecture on the true nature of love when I tell you this, sweet Stacy, but I'm going to brave the storm and tell you anyway," he murmured with a small, faintly wicked quirk to his mouth. His hands stroked leisurely over her body.

"What is this awful confession you're about to make?" she demanded in amusement.

"Only that it was those times when you were in my arms that I dared have any hope of making you love me."

"Thought you could break down my resistance with old-fashioned lust, is that it?" she teased, shivering as his hand moved to her breast and he sensuously thumbed the tip.

"Not exactly," he said with a low, husky laugh. "It was just that you seemed to be able to respond to me so sweetly, so intensely, I began to believe it must mean you felt something for me. On our wedding night—"

"On our wedding night"—she smiled, touching his lips with her fingertip to silence him—"I was determined to show you that you weren't the only one who went a little crazy when we made love. I suppose it was the witch in me challenging the devil in you."

"I tried to restrain myself at first," he admitted. "I think there was a feeling in me that it would be easier to control you, make you respond if I kept a tight rein on myself."

"That ability you have of controlling your temper really annoyed me," she told him. "Then, when it turned out you could control your reaction in bed, also, it was too much! A woman can't let a man have everything his own way, you know."

"Witch," he growled, lowering his head to fasten his mouth over hers. "I've had nothing my own way since the day I met you!" His lips lazed across hers and then traveled along the line of her throat to her breast. His hand began weaving that delicate, enticing pattern on the skin of her stomach and lower, and Stacy moaned softly.

"Tell me you love me, Stacy," he said huskily, caressing her nipple with his tongue.

"I love you, Hunter. I will always love you."

Her fingers began clenching unconsciously in the thick darkness of his hair, and as his hands moved over her she began to arch in response.

"Stacy, my sweet flower witch, I love you so much," he grated. His mouth was beginning to burn on her skin now, and his hands were exploring her warmth with rising urgency.

Stacy's legs shifted temptingly, and Hunter responded by increasing the intimacy of the embrace, letting her feel the male need in him.

"Ah, Hunter," she cried out softly as she clung to him.

"Are you ready to open the garden gate for me?" he whispered passionately, pressing himself close. She felt the strength of him against her hip.

"Oh, yes, please!" she murmured. There would be no teasing games tonight, she realized, only the direct communication of their love and desire for one another. The teasing, the little love games would come later when this new seal on their latest bargain had been established.

Hunter moved, raising himself and closing what little distance remained between them with a fierce, urgent, mastery. He stretched along the length of her, absorbing the feel of his wife from head to toe before establishing the rhythm that would lead them to the top of the familiar spiral.

But Stacy's own urgency was too great to permit any long period of contemplation now that he had completed the embrace. It was she who began to move this time, arching upward with her own wiry strength, making the demands he seemed to find so much satisfaction in fulfilling.

"Hey, flower lady," he said gently, warmly, "I was going to make this slow and gallant and loving . . ."

"Loving, yes," she agreed, green eyes gleaming up at him through her lashes. "By all means, loving . . ."

"Yes," he said, the heat in his eyes flaring into full flame. How could she ever have thought those gray depths cold? "Loving!" He wrapped her deep in the depths of his passion with a sudden forcefulness that made Stacy tremble in response.

After that there were no meaningful words, only the cries and soft sounds of love. Hunter and Stacy, clinging to each other, set sail in the strange and wonderful cosmos known only to lovers. Together they gloried in the ancient, ever-new mysteries that led them from one star-bright planet to another, coming closer and closer to the sun until they fell headfirst into it, letting the fire consume them with total abandon.

At long last Stacy lay quietly in the aftermath of love, tangled in her husband's arms, and smiled dreamily into his love-gentled face.

"What are you thinking, witch?" he asked, playing with a lock of her red-brown hair. "That there is still a devil in me? I've warned you before that you arouse something primitive deep inside me. But I would never willingly hurt you. You must tell me at once if I ever get too carried away—"

"Hunter," she interrupted at once, "you have never hurt me and you know it! The only times I've been even mildly bruised are when I've dragged my heels a little too much—"

"And found yourself hitting the side of your cage?" he finished, chuckling with male satisfaction.

"I can't promise it won't happen again in the future," she told him carefully. "I'm still stuck with a temper that it appears I haven't completely mastered, and I'm still blessed with a full degree of stubbornness." She frowned slightly, wondering if he were under some false impression that her whole personality would change because of her love.

"Trying to frighten me, witch?" he teased, cradling her close, eyes gleaming. "I've told you before, your temper doesn't alarm me. And I've also told you I wouldn't allow you to do yourself any serious injury by battling too ferociously with me. I think we can handle each other, Stacy Manning, don't you?"

She paused, considering that. "Well, I suppose so," she

drawled. "As long as you promise not to resort to brute strength. . . ."

"More bargains, flower lady?" He grinned. "Haven't you learned your lesson yet?"

"Will you promise?" she prodded, hiding her laughter.

"Stacy, beloved, I'm very much in love, but I'm no fool. Don't think you're going to get all the deals you want by waiting to make them until you've weakened me in bed!" She felt the rough humor in him, but she also sensed the underlying strength.

"Pity," she sighed. "I'd hoped I'd found your vulnerable point."

"I'm vulnerable enough as it is around you, witch," he retorted, lying back against the pillow and pulling her across his chest. "Speaking of bargains, darling," he went on in a lazy voice as she ran her fingers lightly through the hair of his chest.

"Umm?"

"I expect this is probably as good a time as any to bring up the little matter of my wedding present. . . ."

"No deal." She grinned at once. "I'm not dumb enough to agree to letting you teach me how to drive it!"

There was a significant pause, and Stacy lifted her eyes to meet his with a sense of curiosity. She could see the considering, waiting look in his face and shook her head warily.

"Oh, no, Hunter," she vowed. "I mean it. I will not have you yelling at me every time I fail to shift properly. I'm sure you'll have absolutely no compassion or sympathy for someone who doesn't have your instinctive feel for machines and hardware."

"That's what you're afraid of? That I won't be patient enough?" he responded, looking quite hurt.

"I'm sure of it!" she declared firmly.

216

He smiled. And Stacy remembered how he had waited coolly for her to return to the house that first night when she had fled him and hidden behind the orchid greenhouse. She remembered how he had waited fourteen years for the revenge that had initially brought him back to Tucson, and she remembered how he had driven her neatly into marriage. Hunter knew all there was to know about bargaining and winning.

"I," he stated, pulling her abruptly close, "am a very patient man. . . ."